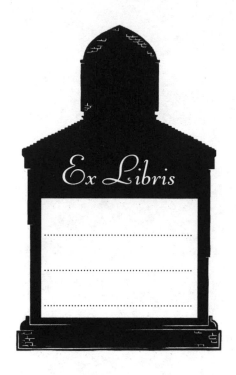

Ex Libris

....

....

The Bonaventure Adventures

RACHELLE
DELANEY

PUFFIN

an imprint of Penguin Canada Books Inc., a Penguin Random House Company

Published by the Penguin Group
Penguin Canada Books Inc., 320 Front Street West, Suite 1400,
Toronto, Ontario M5V 3B6, Canada

Penguin Group (USA) LLC, 375 Hudson Street, New York, New York 10014, U.S.A.
Penguin Books Ltd, 80 Strand, London WC2R ORL, England
Penguin Ireland, 25 St Stephen's Green, Dublin 2, Ireland
(a division of Penguin Books Ltd)
Penguin Group (Australia), 707 Collins Street, Melbourne, Victoria 3008, Australia
(a division of Pearson Australia Group Pty Ltd)
Penguin Books India Pvt Ltd, 11 Community Centre, Panchsheel Park,
New Delhi – 110 017, India
Penguin Group (NZ), 67 Apollo Drive, Rosedale, Auckland 0632, New Zealand
(a division of Pearson New Zealand Ltd)
Penguin Books (South Africa) (Pty) Ltd, 24 Sturdee Avenue,
Rosebank, Johannesburg 2196, South Africa

Penguin Books Ltd, Registered Offices: 80 Strand, London WC2R ORL, England

First published 2017

1 2 3 4 5 6 7 8 9 10 (RRD)

Manufactured in the U.S.A.

Library and Archives Canada Cataloguing in Publication

Delaney, Rachelle, author
The Bonaventure adventures / Rachelle Delaney.

Issued in print and electronic formats.
ISBN 978-0-14-319850-5 (hardback). —ISBN 978-0-14-319852-9 (epub)

I. Title.

PS8607.E48254B66 2017   jC813'.6   C2016-905210-9
                                                 C2016-905211-7

Library of Congress Control Number: 2016948511

Visit the Penguin Canada website at **www.penguinrandomhouse.ca**

Penguin
Random
House

For John Delaney

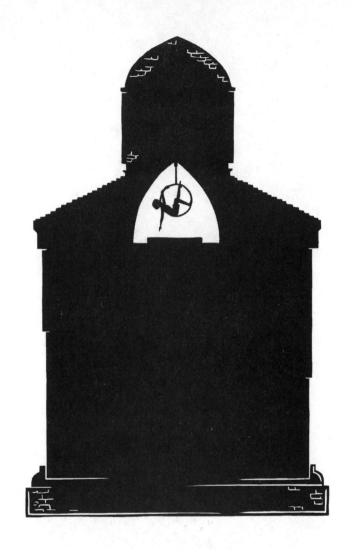

Part 1

IN THE CRIMSON

T HE DAY THAT would later inspire *The Great Adventure*—the circus show that, everyone agreed, changed everything—began like any other.

Sebastian Konstantinov awoke early, the first one in his caravan up, as usual. For a moment he considered changing out of the T-shirt he'd slept in—an old blue one emblazoned with THE KONSTANTINOV FAMILY CIRCUS and so threadbare you could practically see right through it. But he decided against it. None of the Konstantinovs cared what he wore, least of all those he was now going to visit.

Seb brushed his teeth over the little sink as quietly as possible so as not to wake his slumbering roommates. They'd had a particularly rough show the previous night, and he could tell they were still reeling from it, even in their sleep. Maxime the sword swallower was snoring throatily. Juan the contortionist was curled up in a tiny ball on his pillow. And Stanley the clown (known as Snickertoot when he was in character) was testing out jokes in his sleep—something about a sheep walking into a bar. Seb couldn't quite get the details, but he was pretty sure it wasn't funny.

It was a good thing Seb was a sound sleeper.

He peered into the cloudy little mirror above the sink and attempted to flatten his hair, which, as usual, sprang right back up, making him look like he was perpetually caught in a hurricane. Which actually wasn't a bad description of life with the Konstantinov Family Circus.

Resigned, he tiptoed back to his bunk, grabbed the rolled-up map he kept underneath it, then slipped out the door to determine exactly where they were.

He stood for a moment on the steps of the caravan, breathing in the chilly morning air and listening to the twitters of some nearby birds. All around him were craggy valleys and forested hills dotted with red-roofed cottages. He unrolled his map.

It was a handmade affair, one that he and Maxime the sword swallower had been working on for years, documenting their journey back and forth across Eastern Europe. They added anything they found particularly interesting, from Slovenian castles to bookstores in Warsaw to a particularly good sausage cart in Estonia.

He located some craggy valleys and red-roofed cottages on the map, which he vaguely remembered drawing about three years ago, when he had been nine years old, and from that he determined that today, they were in Bulgaria. It made sense, since the previous night they'd dismantled the big top in Bucharest, Romania, and headed south.

"Bulgaria it is, then." Seb rolled up his map and took in his surroundings. The ten caravans, each emblazoned like Seb's T-shirt, had come to rest on the side of an empty gravel road. Everyone inside them seemed to be still asleep, possibly reluctant to face the day after last night's performance.

It wasn't that anyone had messed up: the jugglers hadn't dropped a pin, the lion hadn't nipped its tamer, the contortionist hadn't even thrown out his shoulder. It was, in fact, a good, solid performance.

"Too bad no one showed up to see it," Seb sighed to the red-roofed cottages. He shoved his hands in the pockets of his jeans, recalling the rows of empty seats, an all-too-common sight these days. At the last minute, he had even run off to a nearby playground, arms laden with bags of buttery popcorn, and tried to coerce some local kids to come to the show. But they'd only laughed and chased him away—after relieving him of the popcorn.

"They just don't know what they're missing," Seb told the forested hills. Then he hopped down the steps onto the road. For no matter what had happened the previous night, the animals still needed to be fed. They were counting on him.

He walked along the row of caravans, which weren't actually *real* caravans—at least, not the kind most people pictured when they thought of a traveling circus. These were big metal shipping containers atop old flatbed trucks. But Dragan Konstantinov insisted they be called caravans, since it sounded more circus-y.

Dragan Konstantinov also insisted the caravans travel in a particular order, beginning with his own, since he was the ringmaster. After his came the one Seb shared with Maxime, Stanley and Juan, followed by Aunt Tatiana's caravan, which she shared with Julie the lion tamer and Maria the aerialist. Then came the kitchen caravan and two big containers packed with equipment—everything from the big top to the bleachers. And then came the largest caravan of all, home to an elephant, a lion, a monkey, a dancing bear, some rabbits and a parakeet.

Or rather, the animal caravan *should* have come after the second equipment caravan. But today, it wasn't there.

Seb stopped. Had someone mixed up the order? Dragan would not be pleased when he found out. He shook his head and continued down the line, past a third equipment container, another that housed two jugglers and three acrobats, and finally, the caravan belonging to a small team of workmen and riggers.

He'd reached the end of the line. And the animals were nowhere to be seen.

"What the . . . ?" He turned around and jogged back, counting caravans as he passed them. When he reached his own, he stopped again. "No. Way," he breathed.

Seb spun around again and sprinted down the line, praying that somehow, *somehow* he'd overlooked a shipping container large enough to hold an elephant, a lion, a monkey, a dancing bear, some rabbits and a parakeet. But by the time he reached the last caravan, he knew it was impossible.

The animals were gone.

One of the riggers—a man named Miles—came strolling by just as Seb wailed, "Noooo!"

Miles jumped a good foot off the ground. "What? What?" he cried.

"Where . . . Where are they?" Seb sputtered, waving his arms around.

"Oh. That." Miles bit his lip and looked down at his shoes. "I'm sorry, Seb. We wanted to let you say good-bye, but you were sleeping, and the boss said—"

That was all Seb needed to know. He turned on his heel and sprinted for Dragan Konstantinov's caravan.

He burst in without knocking. His father was sitting before a giant mirror rimmed with tiny lightbulbs—the soft kind he insisted on for the way they illuminated his pores. Currently, he was deep in concentration, parting his thick, shiny pelt of hair, which had always reminded Seb of a large muskrat.

"W-what did y-you . . . ," Seb began, but his throat tightened and the words wouldn't come out.

Dragan's eyes flicked over to his son, then back to his hair. "So you saw, then," he said.

"What did you *do*?" Seb yelled.

Dragan frowned at him in the mirror. "I thought we discussed this."

"Discussed this?" Seb repeated. "*Discussed this!* We definitely did not discuss you getting rid of all our animals!" He was hollering now, quite possibly loud enough to wake the entire Konstantinov family. And he didn't care a bit.

"We did." Dragan gave his pelt a final swipe. "We talked—many times, in fact—about needing to modernize our acts and draw in new audiences. Circus animals," he added, setting down his comb, "have gone out of fashion."

"So you just let them all go?" Seb wailed. "In the middle of the night? In *Romania*?"

"Of course not." Dragan looked insulted. "I sold them to the Bucharest Zoo. And got precious little money for them, by the way," he added. "Honestly, a perfectly good elephant is worth twice what they gave me."

"A zoo?" Seb felt ill. "They're not meant to be in a zoo! They're travelers, like us! Dad, they'll hate it. Especially the lion—you know how she feels about having her photo taken." He grabbed his father's arm. "Let's go back. Please!"

Dragan shook him off and began rummaging through his bag of toiletries. "We are most definitely not going back."

"But you didn't even let me say good-bye!"

"You were sound asleep," said Dragan. "I decided that was more important—we all need our beauty sleep," he added, pulling out his tweezers.

"Dad!" Seb put his head in his hands.

"Oh, stop," said his father. "They're just animals."

"No, they aren't!" Seb thought about how the elephant would snuffle his shoulder with her trunk every morning, as if to thank him for her breakfast. And how the monkey wrapping its long arms around his neck could cheer him up on even the most desolate day. Then he imagined them all, abandoned at the Bucharest Zoo while the caravans sped off into the night. His eyes began to blur. "They were family."

"Nonsense," Dragan sniffed, tweezing his eyebrows.

"It is not!" Seb cried. "They're just as much family as everyone else!" He gestured toward the open door and the caravans beyond, inside which the performers were likely all lying awake, listening to the argument between the ringmaster and his son—the only two Konstantinovs, incidentally, who were actually related.

"I had to do it, Seb," his father said. "Anyway, you're the one who's been encouraging me to modernize."

"But not like this!" said Seb. "Not by selling off our performers! I said we need to—"

"Don't start with the stories again," said Dragan.

"I *will* start with the stories again!" Seb shot back. "There are great shows out there that—"

"Enough!" Dragan held up his tweezers for silence. "This is not a matter of . . . of storytelling." He grimaced. "This is about performances—about showcasing only the most talented and skilled Konstantinovs." He gave Seb a pointed look—a look that clearly said, "You're not exactly helping with that."

Seb flinched. Even after all these years, it still hurt.

For a moment, they just stared at each other, pores illuminated by all the tiny lightbulbs. Then Dragan opened his mouth, likely to apologize. But before he could say another word, Seb turned and stomped out of the caravan.

S EB STORMED BACK down the road, keeping his eyes on the gravel so everyone he passed would know he was in no mood to talk.

Abandoned! At a zoo! He couldn't believe it. It was by far the most unfair thing his father had ever done. And that look he'd given him—the "you're not helping" look. *That* was a low blow.

"I help," Seb grumbled, stomping past the kitchen caravan where Aunt Tatiana was cooking her usual giant pot of porridge. He left the road and marched out onto a patch of grass, then sat down with his back to the caravans. "I do all kinds of things around here."

And Dragan knew that. What he had meant by that look, and all the looks over the years, was that Seb wasn't—would never be—a circus performer.

It certainly wasn't for lack of trying. Seb had spent the better part of his life attempting to master every circus skill imaginable, from juggling to trapeze to tying his limbs in a knot. But it was no use. He was terrible at everything circus-y.

He understood why it was hard for his father. Dragan had been a world-renowned aerialist before founding the Konstantinov Family Circus—of course he'd assumed his son would be just as talented. Or at least decent. Or at least able to turn a simple cartwheel without ending up in a heap on the floor.

To his credit, Dragan had never actually come out and said he was disappointed in his son. But Seb knew. He'd known ever since the day he found the letters.

He'd first come upon them about a year before, shortly after the Konstantinovs had finally, mercifully given up on the prospect of him ever being a circus star. They'd begun to give him odd jobs instead, like mucking out the animal stalls and popping popcorn for the shows. On this particular day, he'd been tasked with fetching a top hat from Dragan's costume closet.

"The one with the teal-green sequins," his father had specified, for he owned at least a dozen top hats.

Seb had been rooting through Dragan's vast collection of spangled scarves, bowties and suspenders when he happened upon a small stack of letters, tied together with twine. It was the paper that first caught his eye—a nice, heavy cardstock, smooth to the touch. Paper, like books and a decent Internet connection, was hard to come by in the Konstantinov Family Circus.

At first, he'd assumed they were from his mother, and he wondered how long ago she'd sent them. He hesitated a moment before untying the twine, then decided it really *was* his business. He pulled on the bow and unfolded the first page.

The letters, it turned out, were not from his mother, but they were from a woman. A woman named, according to her swirling signature, Angélique Saint-Germain. Disappointed, Seb was about to fold the paper back up when he spotted something of interest.

I want so badly to meet Sebastian, Madame Saint-Germain had written. *I do hope you'll send him to us, even just for a visit.*

"Who's us?" Seb asked his father's accessories. They offered no explanation. So he shut the door, sat down on the floor and pulled out the flashlight he always kept in his pocket to use backstage. And he began to read the letters, one by one.

As he made his way through them—there were about a dozen, sent over six months earlier that year—he began to piece together the story. Like Dragan, Angélique Saint-Germain had been a circus aerial star. At one time they'd even trained together on the flying trapeze. In her first letter, Madame Saint-Germain went on at length, reminiscing about competitions they'd won and performers they'd outshone.

We were quite the pair, weren't we, Dragan? she wrote. *With my talent and your charisma, it seemed we could take on the world.*

Charisma was the word everyone used to describe Dragan. Seb had looked it up long ago and found it to mean "charm that inspires devotion in others." He couldn't argue with that: each time his father entered a room, everyone in it inevitably turned to revolve around him. Seb had seen it happen time and time again, while he himself blended nicely into the walls.

Women, especially, loved Dragan. Whether it was due to the charisma or his well-groomed muskrat pelt or his meticulously plucked eyebrows, Seb couldn't say for sure. But whatever it was, it inspired devotion in all women who met him. With the exception, of course, of Seb's mother.

He knew very little else about his mother. When he was small, he used to ask Dragan why she'd left the Konstantinov Family Circus. But each time he did, his father had a different story. She went off to pursue her dream of dental school. She fell from a tightrope and developed a paralyzing fear of heights. Tired of Aunt Tatiana's goulash, she left one day in search of a croissant and never returned.

For someone so opposed to storytelling, Dragan was basically a master.

Unfortunately, Dragan was also the kind of storyteller whose stories were most often untrue. Over the years, Seb had developed a trick to telling when his father was making things up: he'd assume his deep, booming ringmaster voice and wave his arms around, as if telling the story to an entire rapt audience, not just a dubious twelve-year-old.

Eventually Seb gave up asking about his mother, for in the end, he told himself, it didn't really matter. She was simply no longer devoted to the charismatic ringmaster and his less-than-charismatic son. She'd chosen a life without them.

Had Angélique Saint-Germain been in love with Dragan? he wondered. He concluded it likely, and read on.

Sebastian Konstantinov! she wrote in one letter. *What a fine name. A name destined for greatness!*

Seb snorted. She clearly had no idea.

He must be eleven years old now, she went on. *Are you training him in acrobatics? Aerials? Please don't say he's a contortionist. You know how I feel about contortionists.*

Then she went on to describe the school she'd founded in Montreal, which Seb believed was a city in Canada—it definitely wasn't on his homemade map. She aimed to fill it with only the most promising young circus stars.

For who better to shape the minds and bodies of the next great performers than Angélique Saint-Germain? she wrote.

Seb was beginning to understand why she and his father had gotten along so well.

But Dragan seemed to have resisted her requests to send Seb for a visit.

You're holding out on me, she wrote in one of her final letters. *I know Sebastian is a rising star—no son of yours could be anything but. First-year students at my circus school are usually twelve years old, but I would make an exception for such a talent. Please send him.*

Only then did it occur to Seb that his father wasn't telling her the truth: that his son didn't have an ounce of talent for circus skills. Likely, he couldn't bring himself to admit it—he was that ashamed. The realization made Seb's stomach sink, and he almost abandoned the letters altogether. But there was only one more to read, so he unfolded it.

You want to keep his talent to yourself, Angélique accused Dragan. *While I suppose I understand this, you must know that the circus world is changing. The shows created today aren't like the one you trot around Eastern Europe.*

"Yes!" Seb whispered in the darkness of the closet. "Tell him," he urged Angélique Saint-Germain. "Tell him about the stories!"

But she didn't mention stories. Instead, she said, *Dragan, you owe your son—the heir to your company—an education in the ways of the modern circus. Think about it, and if you ever have a change of heart, you may contact my Scout at the address below.*

Seb folded the letter back up, wondering whether he should tell his father that he'd read it and all the others. But what good would that do? And anyway, the letters hadn't been his to read.

So he tied them back up, tucked them under a pile of tasseled epaulettes, and did his best to forget them.

3

LARGELY, HE HAD succeeded. In fact, Seb barely thought about the letters again until a few days after the animals were abandoned at the Bucharest Zoo.

He hadn't spoken to Dragan since he'd stormed out of his caravan. So when Maxime the sword swallower found him in their own caravan one evening and asked him to come to an important family meeting, Seb couldn't help but groan.

"I'm really busy," he said, pointing to the mystery novel he was rereading for the thirteenth time. It was part of a small collection he kept hidden under his bed, as his father had a tendency to use books for other purposes, like propping up tables and lining animal cages.

"Come on." Maxime sat down on Seb's narrow bunk. "You can't not speak to him forever."

Seb looked up from the novel and considered this. "I probably could," he said.

"Yeah," Maxime agreed, for Maxime was very agreeable. "You probably could. But what good would it do?"

"Maybe he'd regret abandoning our animals," Seb grunted.

"*Ah bien.*" Maxime sighed. "I know it's been a hard week for you. But I bet the animals are doing fine. They're . . . how do you say . . . *entreprenants.*"

"Resourceful," said Seb. Maxime hailed from Marseilles and had taught Seb quite a bit of French over the years. "I guess so," he said, though he wasn't sure how resourcefulness would help them in the zoo. Unless, say, the monkey used his lock-picking skills to bust out of his cage, then freed his circus friends. Seb pictured them all sneaking out onto the dark streets of Bucharest and making a break for the countryside. It made him smile—but only for a moment, for it was just a story. It didn't change what had happened.

"They aren't doing fine," he snapped, picking up his book again. "They're miserable, I know it. They feel betrayed."

Maxime sighed and folded his hands in his lap. "I'm sorry, Seb. I wish I could make it better."

Seb lowered his book again. "It's not your fault," he grumbled, for there was no point in making Maxime feel bad about it. Maxime was his favorite Konstantinov. Not only did he take time to teach Seb French and work on his homemade map of Eastern Europe, but also he'd brought him to the show that had changed everything for Seb.

It happened about four months prior, while they were traveling through Russia and found themselves in Saint Petersburg with two entire days off. Maxime suggested they hop a fast train to Finland, just on a whim. And so, a mere four hours later, he and Seb disembarked in the seaside city of Helsinki. As devoted circophiles (a word Maxime had taught him, which meant "circus lovers"), they immediately went to see a show.

But this wasn't just any old circus show. There was no big top, no animals, no tinny orchestral music—just a few dozen chairs arranged in a circle in a tiny theater with stark white walls. Seb had just begun to question whether they were in the right place when two men appeared onstage, dressed in jeans and T-shirts. Now Seb was certain they'd come to the wrong show. But before he could tell Maxime, the men launched into their performance.

Like actors in a play, they told the story of two brothers torn apart by a feuding family, only to find each other years later while fighting in a war, in opposing armies. Except they told the entire story through circus acts. They acted out their teenage antics through a hand-balancing routine, one man perched atop the other.

To show their frustration at being separated, they did a ropes routine, climbing and twisting and dropping from daring heights.

And when they met again during the war, the men pulled a giant teeterboard onstage and began to bounce on either end of it, flipping each other higher and higher with such intensity that Seb nearly stopped breathing. When the show ended, his knees were almost too weak to give them a standing ovation. Almost.

He'd probably thanked Maxime four hundred times for that trip to Helsinki. And for teaching him that a different kind of circus existed—one that involved stories.

Now Seb sat up and slipped his novel back under the bed. "Okay, fine, I'll come to the meeting."

"*Courage, mon vieux.*" Maxime took his hand and pulled him up. "Family is important. Both the family you're born into and the family you choose."

"Yeah, I guess." Seb sighed. "Hey, Max?"

"Yep."

"I'm glad you chose to be a Konstantinov." In fact, there was no one else he would have preferred as a fake brother.

Max grinned. "Me too, Seb." He clapped him on the shoulder and steered him toward the door.

INSIDE HIS CARAVAN, Dragan had set up a card table and a few folding chairs, as he always did for family meetings. When Seb and Maxime entered, they found him seated at the table, flanked by Stanley the clown and Juan the contortionist. Dragan gave Seb a wary look. Seb looked away.

A minute later, Julie the lion tamer slunk in and took her place as well. Exactly what she would do now that the lion was behind bars in Bucharest had yet to be determined. Possibly that was a topic on the meeting agenda.

"Well, then," said Dragan, "let's get started."

"Wait," said Seb. "Where's Aunt Tatiana?"

"Not coming," Dragan replied.

"What? Why?" asked Seb. Tatiana had been one of the very first members of the Konstantinov Family Circus; she never missed a family meeting. Dragan waved away the question, which Seb decided was not a good sign. He pushed his chair back from the table and folded his arms across his chest.

"As you've likely guessed, this family meeting is about finances," Dragan began. He nodded at Stanley, who pulled out his reading glasses and some spreadsheets. Stanley had been an accountant in New Jersey before joining the Konstantinovs.

"Things are looking dire," he reported. "We're in the red. Like, really in the red. Scarlet, you might say."

"Or crimson?" Maxime suggested. "Is crimson darker than scarlet?"

"A shade or two," Juan confirmed. He'd been a cosmetologist in Barcelona before joining the Konstantinovs.

"Anyway," Stanley sighed, "the point is we're losing money."

"But now we don't have to feed the animals," Dragan pointed out. "We've cut costs there. That must help."

"Not enough," said Stanley. "It barely saves us anything."

"So what you're saying is," Seb cut in, "there was no point in getting rid of the animals."

"Yes, there was," Dragan snapped. "We need to modernize our acts. And circus animals have gone—"

"Out of fashion." Seb rolled his eyes. "Right." Of course, he knew Dragan was right; modern circus shows rarely involved animals. But it still wasn't fair. Once again he brought to mind an image of the monkey springing all the animals free and leading them off into the night. It made him feel a bit better, even if it was just a story.

Dragan pulled out a notebook. "The fact remains, we need to take new measures." He flipped the book open. "So I've come up with some options."

"Let's hear 'em." Stanley leaned back in his chair and put his giant red shoes up on the table.

"Option one," Dragan began. "We leave Eastern Europe and head someplace new. Australia, maybe. Or Zimbabwe."

"Can't afford it." Stanley shook his head. "We're in the red, remember?"

"In the crimson," offered Maxime. He elbowed Seb. "That's poetic, isn't it?"

"It's not bad," Seb agreed.

Dragan gave them the stink-eye. "Option two. We rebrand. Get a new logo. Maybe a catchy acronym—we could be the KFC."

"I think that one's taken," Seb pointed out.

Dragan struck it off his list. "Option three, then." He leaned forward on the table. "We get rid of another act that's gone out of fashion."

"Ah." Julie the lion tamer nodded. "You mean the contortionist."

"Hey, he's right here!" Stanley exclaimed. "Have a little compassion!"

"Is it me?" Juan paled.

"Of course not," Dragan said impatiently. "I'm thinking about the bearded lady."

"What!" Seb cried. "Not Aunt Tatiana!"

"Bearded ladies," Dragan declared, "have gone out of fashion."

"But she's family!" Seb protested.

"And she makes the most delicious goulash," Juan added.

"And she gets the mail," Julie pointed out.

The Konstantinovs murmured in agreement. Over the years, Aunt Tatiana had established an elaborate system of mail delivery, which involved letters being shipped from the Konstantinovs' main post office box in Prague to various people she knew around the continent. It was highly complicated, but Dragan insisted on it, on the off-chance that he received some glowing fan mail.

"Maybe you could take care of the mail," Stanley said to Julie. "What else have you got going on now?"

"I'm taking up the unicycle," she informed him, then looked at Dragan, who nodded. "Apparently, it's back in fashion."

"The point is, Aunt Tatiana is *family!*" Seb repeated, thumping the table for emphasis.

Dragan threw up his hands. "Well then, you come up with a better option!"

Seb sat back and took a deep breath. Aunt Tatiana had been like a mother to him, ever since his own had left for dental school or a baguette or whatever. He pictured Aunt Tatiana left by the side of the road, her beard still in its bedtime curlers, as the caravans sped off into the night . . .

It made him feel like he'd been stabbed by one of Maxime's duller swords (which actually had happened on a few occasions—when you bunked with a sword swallower, it was pretty well inevitable).

"Just . . . just wait," he said, trying to keep his voice steady. "There has to be a way to modernize the circus without getting rid of any more Konstantinovs. What about—"

"Stories are not a solution," Dragan warned.

Seb closed his mouth.

As soon as he and Maxime had returned from Helsinki, Seb had beelined for Dragan's caravan to regale his father with all he'd seen.

"Circus and stories together, Dad!" he'd said dreamily. "It's the best of everything. Imagine if we were to create shows that were more like plays, but with circus acts. We'd sell more tickets, I just know we would."

Dragan, however, had only sniffed. "The Konstantinov Family Circus is keeping the traditional circus alive," he'd informed Seb. "When you have talented and skilled performers, you don't need to distract the audience with stories."

And to Seb's great surprise and utter disappointment, he wouldn't hear another word about it.

"He doesn't get it," Seb had later lamented to Maxime. "I bet he's never seen a show like that."

"I'm sure he has," Maxime had replied. "But he's never created one, so he's probably scared of the idea. Plus," he added, "modern circuses don't usually have ringmasters."

"But ours could," Seb argued. "We'd have a role for everyone, so no one would be left out. I'm sure we could come up with something great."

Maxime had agreed. But neither of them had been able to convince Dragan.

If only there were some way to make him see that the circus world is changing, Seb now thought, staring at his father across the card table. That modern shows weren't like the one they toured around Eastern Europe.

Then he paused, for those words sounded oddly familiar.

And he remembered the letters.

4

DEAR MR. SCOUT,
I have decided to take Madame Saint-Germain up on her offer to attend the Bonaventure Circus School.

Seb paused, tapping his pen on his chin. Did that sound presumptuous? What if they'd been annoyed when they hadn't heard from Dragan? What if they'd forgotten about Seb altogether? He crumpled the paper and pulled out a fresh sheet from the small stack in his father's caravan, where he sat before the pore-illuminating mirror. He had to be careful not to waste it.

Since the family meeting two days prior, Seb had managed to steal a bit of time on Stanley's laptop, and he'd learned a few important things about Angélique Saint-Germain's circus school. First, he'd learned its name: the Bonaventure Circus School. He quite liked that. It sounded like an adventure.

Second, he learned that the city of Montreal was indeed in Canada—in a province called Quebec, where most everyone spoke French. This, too, felt promising, thanks to Maxime's lessons.

Third, he learned that most students attended Bonaventure for four years, until they were sixteen years old and ready to join a professional circus company. This sounded reasonable to Seb; four years would give him enough time to find a way to save the Konstantinovs.

However, he also learned a fourth, not-so-promising thing: that any student wanting to attend Bonaventure had to audition. And according to the website, competition was fierce.

There was no denying it; if Seb had to audition, it would be all over. He still cringed to think of his failed attempts at mastering circus skills, not to mention all the Konstantinovs he'd let down. The last thing he wanted to do was relive that.

But if for some reason he could get around it . . . If, say, he penned a really persuasive letter . . .

He bent over his paper and tried again.

Dear Mr. Scout,

I'm Sebastian Konstantinov, of the Konstantinov Family Circus. About a year ago, Angélique Saint-Germain

generously offered to let me attend the Bonaventure
Circus School, and I hope that offer still stands.

He paused and read what he'd written. It was good, he decided. He pushed on.

HE POSTED HIS letter in Sofia, the biggest city in Bulgaria (and featured prominently on his homemade map). He mailed it himself rather than handing it off to Aunt Tatiana, for she would have wanted an explanation, and he wasn't ready to talk about it. For one thing, he knew the Konstantinovs would flip out when they discovered he'd applied for school halfway around the world. But most important, talking about what he'd done would make it real—not just an idea in his head. And when it was real, he'd actually have to consider what life would be like at a circus school halfway around the world, without any Konstantinovs for company.

He wasn't ready for reality yet.

He didn't know what to expect after posting the letter. He might never hear back from the Scout at all. Or he might receive a rejection, a thanks-but-no-thanks. There was also a chance that the Scout would want to arrange an audition, or request a video demonstrating Seb's skills. And in that case, it would be all over. This was another reason not to tell the Konstantinovs what he'd done: there was no sense in getting them all excited only to have everyone's hopes dashed.

Fortunately, he didn't have to wait long to find out his fate. The answer arrived a mere two weeks later, during an impromptu afternoon rehearsal. The Konstantinovs had just set up in a small town across the Serbian border, and no one knew quite what to expect from ticket sales. In an attempt to get everyone's mind off their troubles, Dragan had called a rehearsal.

Seb had his doubts that a rehearsal would raise people's spirits, but he was always happy to watch. He stationed himself in one of the wings, where he could see everything onstage and off.

Onstage, Dragan was parading around in his favorite teal top hat, waving his arms and bellowing at an imaginary audience about the most talented family on earth, whose feats they were about to witness. Backstage, the three acrobats were limbering up their shoulders and practicing their splits. The aerialist was dusting her hands with resin so she didn't slip from the silks. Nearby, two riggers were discussing the state of the bolts keeping the trapeze from tumbling down onto the stage.

If only the audiences could see what went on backstage, Seb thought, not for the first time. The nerves, the excitement, the bruises and tears, the way everyone came together no matter what, to make sure the show went on. Maybe then they'd understand the magic. Maybe then they'd buy tickets, and the Konstantinovs wouldn't have to worry about—

Someone tapped his elbow, and he looked up to see Aunt Tatiana. She was wearing a long dressing gown over her costume, and her beard was woven into an intricate braid.

"What's up?" he asked.

"Thought you'd be hungry," she said, passing him a square of gingerbread cake. His stomach rumbled in agreement. He took a giant bite.

"Thank you," he said over a mouthful. Onstage, Dragan announced the first act, and the acrobats burst into the ring in a frenzy of flips and cartwheels.

"Also, I just got the mail," said Aunt Tatiana.

"Oh yeah?" Seb swallowed his gingerbread, put two fingers in his mouth, and whistled at the acrobats.

"Here," said Tatiana, and Seb tore his gaze away from the ring. She was holding out an envelope. "It's from Montreal."

"Oh!" he exclaimed.

"What's in Montreal?" asked Tatiana.

"Oh. Um." He took the letter. "Can I tell you later?"

She regarded him for a moment, then nodded and walked away.

Seb held the envelope up to the light. It was indeed addressed to him, on a nice, heavy cardstock that was smooth to the touch.

"Wow," he breathed. His stomach turned a backflip.

Onstage, the acrobats were building a wobbly tower with folding chairs. Soon, he knew, they would climb up onto it and use it as a precarious diving board for their flips and tumbles. It was Seb's favorite part of their routine, and it would be followed by Maxime and his swords, then the contortionist's new act, in which he attempted to fit himself into a guitar case.

But Seb couldn't possibly concentrate on the rehearsal, not with his fate right there in his hands.

"Sorry, guys," he whispered to the acrobats. And he hurried out of the big top and down the row of caravans until he reached his own. He ducked behind it and sank down in the grass near one of the rear tires.

Then he took a deep breath, tore open the envelope, and unfolded the letter.

It read:

Dear Sebastian,

On behalf of our esteemed directrice, Angélique Saint-Germain, I would like to welcome you to the Bonaventure Circus School. We are thrilled that you have accepted our offer to attend. Madame Saint-Germain speaks very highly of your father and is certain that a descendant of Dragan Konstantinov—and heir to the Konstantinov Family Circus—will be an excellent addition to Bonaventure.

We are, therefore, delighted to offer you a full scholarship, including room and board, at the school in beautiful Old Montreal.

The school year begins September 1, in two months' time, and out-of-town students typically arrive a day or two early. I will make all travel arrangements for you, including your flight and airport pickup in Montreal. You have only to tell me where in the world you'll be in late August.

Congratulations, Sebastian, on making the excellent decision to study at the Bonaventure Circus School. We so look forward to meeting you in person.

Sincerely,
Michel Letourneau
Bonaventure Circus School Scout

★ ★ ★

AN HOUR LATER, Seb was still pacing around the caravans, too nervous to sit still.

"I've been accepted. Into circus school," he told himself for the perhaps the thirty-seventh time. "I did it. They let me in." Even when he said it aloud, it didn't seem like it could possibly be true.

He pulled out the letter and checked it again, front and back. There was no mention at all of an audition. Which meant they assumed he had circus skills.

Which made him feel a little bit faint.

He was just about to sit back down when Stanley appeared. Or rather, Snickertoot appeared, for Stanley was in clown mode, dressed in a tattered red suit jacket, baggy blue trousers and massive red shoes, and wearing a spongy red ball on his nose.

"Heya, kid." He jingled his shoes at Seb. "I've been looking for you. You had dinner yet?"

Seb shook his head. There was no way he could eat.

"Well, we need you to round up some locals. We've only sold a few tickets, and your dad's getting all . . . you know." Snickertoot bared his teeth and raised his shoulders up to his ears.

"Got it," said Seb.

"Here are some flyers." The clown handed him a small stack. "Draw in some crowds for us, will ya?"

Seb glanced down at the flyers, which featured scenes from the show: Maxime swallowing a sword, the clown tripping over his pant legs, the acrobats diving from their tower of chairs. And of course, Dragan Konstantinov, front and center. He had his arm looped around the lion, who looked less than thrilled to have her photo taken.

"Kind of false advertising, isn't it?" Seb said. "Since we don't have the lion anymore."

Snickertoot shrugged. "So tell them she's sick. Make something up. You like stories."

Seb decided against reminding him that he didn't speak Serbian. He nodded and pocketed the flyers, and the clown waddled away.

As Seb watched him go, red shoes jingling, he was suddenly struck by an overwhelming sense of "What have I *done*?" In two months' time, he'd be leaving his family and moving halfway around the world to a city he knew absolutely nothing about.

What would Montreal be like? he wondered. Who would his friends be? Would he even have any friends?

Really, he only knew one thing for certain.

His father was going to kill him.

Or at the very least, Dragan would be very, very upset.

The Konstantinovs had never been allowed to make changes without consulting him first. Maxime couldn't swap a cutlass for a bayonet, even though he was the one coaxing them down his throat. The aerialist couldn't add any new tricks to her performance. Tatiana couldn't even toss a new ingredient into the goulash without Dragan's okay. His twelve-year-old son's plan to move halfway around the world to study the modern circus was not going to go over well.

But it was, Seb reminded himself, for the good of all the Konstantinovs. It was the only plan they had that just might work. And so he resumed pacing, considering the ways in which he could break the news.

Option one, he decided, was to not tell anyone what he'd done. He'd simply steal off into the night, board a plane to Montreal and send Dragan a postcard once he'd arrived safe and sound.

But even Seb, who'd never boarded a plane in his life, knew that the likelihood of a kid flying transcontinental without adult supervision was basically zero. Option one, appealing as it was, would never work.

Option two involved waiting until after that night's performance, then breaking the news to his father. But if crowds were as sparse in Serbia as they'd been in Bulgaria, Dragan would be in a foul mood. Plus, Seb didn't think his own nerves could wait that long.

"I guess it's option three, then," he decided. He would tell his father then and there.

He found Dragan in his caravan again, sitting in front of his mirror while Juan the contortionist did his makeup.

"Hi, Dad." Seb closed the door behind him.

Dragan looked at him, then closed his eyes so Juan could powder his face. "Is this about the animals again?"

"No," Seb said. "Not this time."

Dragan waved at him to proceed.

Seb cleared his throat. "I have a plan," he said. "To save the circus."

Dragan opened one eye and looked over at him. Juan tsked and turned his head back. He began tracing Dragan's left eyelid with black liner.

"It's . . . it's not going to be a quick fix," Seb went on. "It'll take a few years. Okay, maybe four. But if we can hang on that long . . ."

"Stop," Dragan commanded Juan, then turned again to stare at Seb. "What are you talking about?"

Seb took a breath. "I want to . . . I mean, I'm *going* to . . . circus school. To study the modern circus."

Juan's eyeliner clattered to the floor.

"It won't cost anything," Seb hurried on. "I have a full scholarship. I . . . I already got accepted. Sorry . . . for not telling you when I applied."

For a moment, Dragan only blinked at him. He opened and closed his mouth a few times, then managed to ask, "To which school?"

Seb swallowed. "Bonaventure."

Juan gasped. "In Paris?"

"Montreal," said Seb.

He cocked his head to one side. "Is that near Paris?"

Seb shook his head. "It's in Canada."

Juan gasped again, this time in horror.

"Leave us," Dragan told him.

"But . . ." Juan gestured to Dragan's half-lined eyes, but the ringmaster waved him off. He let himself out in a huff.

Dragan sighed and rubbed his forehead, getting powder on his fingers. "How did she find you?"

"She didn't," Seb told him. "I found the letters in your closet about a year ago. I was looking for a hat or something. But I wasn't snooping," he added.

Dragan closed his eyes and groaned.

"Look, I think it's a good idea," Seb went on. "I can come back every summer to tell you what I've learned. It might not even take me all four years to figure it out. Just . . . just please don't get rid of anyone else until I come back. Okay? Promise?"

Dragan folded his hands in his lap and turned to his mirror, frowning at his reflection. He looked suddenly old, Seb realized. Or maybe the lightbulbs were on the fritz.

"Seb," he sighed, "you can't go to circus school."

"Yes, I can," Seb insisted. "They're giving me a full scholarship, with room and board. It won't cost us anything."

"Seb," Dragan said seriously, "you'll have to take skills classes. And you have no skills."

"Oh." Seb flinched a little. "Right."

"You can't juggle to save your life," Dragan went on. "You can't turn a flip, or even a somersault. You can't pull yourself up onto a trapeze. The last time you tried to climb the silks, you got so tangled we had to cut you down! Don't you remember?"

"Yes," said Seb, who had no desire to relive that scene.

"You're really, *really* bad!" Dragan still sounded incredulous after all these years. "At *everything!*"

"Okay, Dad. I get it," said Seb.

Dragan sighed. "Sorry. But Seb, there's bound to be an audition. They won't let you in without testing your skills."

"Apparently they will." Seb pulled the Scout's letter out of his pocket and handed it to his father.

Dragan read it over, then groaned again. "Sebastian," he said, "I have been in the circus business long enough to know this is a bad idea."

Seb shrugged. "Do you have a better one?"

For a moment, Dragan just stared at him through the mirror. Then he heaved a sigh. "Have I ever told you about Angélique Saint-Germain?"

Seb shook his head.

"Well, I'd better." He motioned for Seb to pull up a chair.

"Angélique Saint-Germain," he began, tenting his fingers in front of his face, "is a very big deal. She was one of the most talented aerialists of our time. She won the Grand Prix at the World Circus Fair five years in a row, and at the Festival Mondial du Cirque three times. She has traveled the world, performed for kings and queens. She even dated the man who played James Bond. You know, the one with the accent?" Dragan stared off into space for a moment.

Seb studied his father for some sign that he was making up another story, but he wasn't using his ringmaster voice or waving his hands around. He waited.

"And she's beautiful," Dragan went on. "I fell in love with her myself, ages ago. But Angélique . . ." He paused again. "Loved another man."

"Instead of you?" Seb couldn't imagine it.

Dragan raised an eyebrow as if to say, "I know, right?"

"She was in love," he said, "with Jean-Loup."

The name was familiar; Seb tried to place it.

"The founder of Terra Incognito."

"Oh, right." Seb nodded. He'd heard about the circus company that staged daring performances "where no circus has gone before," like beneath the sea in giant submarines and in Borneon bat caves. "The guy with the monocle." Jean-Loup was also known for his old-fashioned eyepiece, which his devoted fans apparently wore in homage at his shows.

"The guy with the monocle." Dragan nodded grimly. "And more money than God."

"So Angélique Saint-Germain doesn't perform anymore?" Seb asked.

Dragan shook his head. "Around the time you were born, she suffered a tremendous fall," he said. "Plummeted from her swinging trapeze, thanks to faulty rigging. But she was so good, so talented, that somehow, she managed to land on her feet. Though she shattered both ankles on impact."

"Yikes!"

Dragan nodded. "Her career was over. She went into hiding for six months, in a castle high in the Carpathian Mountains, owned by none other than Jean-Loup. When she emerged, she had reinvented herself as the directrice of a new circus school." He paused. "I suppose I should have told you when she first wrote, asking for you."

Seb swallowed. "I get why you didn't."

Dragan regarded him for a moment. "Sebastian, are you sure you want to do this?" he asked. "I know Angélique. She will not be forgiving of someone who isn't naturally skilled."

"I figured that," said Seb. "But I'm . . . I'm working on a plan."

Dragan raised an eyebrow. "Care to share?"

"It's still in progress," Seb said. Actually, it was still just a half-formed idea. He had some serious work to do.

Dragan grunted. For a minute or two, they both fell silent. Then Seb said, "I've been thinking about the fire breather. Remember him?"

His father nodded.

The fire breather had been an impressive act, though short-lived, as he'd fallen in love with an ice dancer when they passed through Saint Petersburg, and decided to stay put.

"I'm really more of a family man," the fire breather had explained.

"He was weird," Dragan recalled.

"Yeah," Seb agreed. "But he once told me that whenever he got nervous, he'd stop and say to himself, 'Okay, I might get hurt here, but what would happen if I didn't even try?'"

Dragan considered this. "Well, he would still have his eyebrows, for one thing."

"True," said Seb. "But he also wouldn't know he could do it, right?"

Dragan shrugged. "But eyebrows."

Seb sighed. "Can I go, Dad?"

Dragan rubbed his temples. "I can't believe I'm even considering this."

"Me neither," said Seb. And despite everything, he had to chuckle. "'Cause I'm, like, really bad!"

Dragan nodded in wonder. "You really are."

They stared at each other in the mirror. And suddenly, they both began to laugh.

"Remember my trampoline lesson?" Seb snorted.

Dragan hooted. "You bounced right off and got caught in the ceiling rafters!"

They laughed until Dragan's eyeliner ran down his cheek and they had to call in the contortionist, who gasped in horror at the sight.

It made them laugh even more.

5

"**Y**OU GUYS DON'T all have to come in," Seb said as the car pulled up in front of the Budapest airport on a muggy afternoon at the very end of August. "I'm sure I can find my way around."

He turned in the passenger seat to see them all squished together on the rear bench: Aunt Tatiana and Maxime, plus Stanley the clown, Juan the contortionist and Julie the unicyclist-in-training. When they'd rented the car earlier that day, they'd been warned that the backseat only fit three. But no one wanted to stay behind, and Juan volunteered to ride in the glove box if need be. So in they'd squeezed, for the momentous occasion of Seb's departure.

"We're coming in," Stanley declared. "We wouldn't miss this."

Out they tumbled, all seven of them, onto the sidewalk in front of the airport. They left the car in the waiting lane, which Seb didn't think was a great idea, but neither did he want to argue. He popped the hatch and pulled out a leather trunk that contained all his worldly possessions. It was, unsurprisingly, quite light. It was also falling apart at the seams. He had a feeling this was symbolic, but didn't really want to ponder it.

"Ready?" Dragan asked, and Seb looked up to see his father watching him. His hair part was crooked, a sure sign he was unsettled.

Seb knew that if he tried to answer, he'd say something like, "No! I'm terrified. What the heck was I thinking? This was the worst idea in the world." Instead, he nodded.

They trooped into the airport. Seb was relieved to see that Maxime had left his swords at home. He only wished he could say the same for Stanley's gigantic red shoes. He'd even worn the jingly bells, for Pete's sake! Everyone was staring.

Seb tried not to be annoyed. It was, he reminded himself, the last time he'd see any of them for ages.

He tried once again to imagine life without the Konstantinov Family Circus. Without watching his favorite people do incredible tricks every night. Without the smells of trodden dirt and cigarette smoke and buttered popcorn. Without tinny orchestral music and Tatiana's goulash and Maxime's throaty snores that kept him company when he woke during the night.

Suddenly, Seb realized that he was standing, frozen, just inside the airport doors. He hurried after his family.

He and Dragan nudged through the crowds until they found the airline the Scout had booked with. He'd arranged everything, just as he'd promised, so Seb only had to set his luggage on a conveyor belt and wait for the attendant who would accompany him to the gate.

Dragan stood beside him, untying and retying his scarf. "You don't have to go, you know," he told Seb.

Seb swallowed. "I already checked in my luggage," he pointed out.

"We can get it back. It's not too late." Dragan looked like he wanted to leap onto the conveyor belt after the trunk.

"It's going to be okay, Dad," Seb said. "I'm going to learn all I can. I'll report back every week." It made him feel slightly better to remind himself of his mission and the prospect of returning someday, triumphant.

Dragan watched the trunk being swept away. Then he looked at Seb. "You won't tell Angélique . . . anyone . . . about the Konstantinovs, will you?"

"What about us?" asked Seb.

"Well, first off, that we're . . ." Dragan glanced around, then lowered his voice, "not related."

Seb looked over his shoulder at the Spanish contortionist, the French sword swallower and the clown from New Jersey, who had begun to wheel around on a luggage cart. He turned back to his father. "You don't think she might have guessed that already?"

Dragan frowned. "Sebastian, this is very important. I've spent decades building the story of the Konstantinovs. You mustn't tell her."

"Okay, okay," said Seb.

"And more important," his father went on, "do not tell her or anyone else about our financial situation. That is a family matter. Do you understand?"

Seb nodded. "I won't."

"Good," Dragan said, but he was still frowning.

"It's going to be okay, Dad," Seb repeated. And because a lump was forming in his throat, he decided not to prolong things.

"Guys, I'm going," he called to the Konstantinovs, who were pulling doughnuts on the luggage cart.

Aunt Tatiana hurried over to hug him, and he buried his face in her beard. Maxime offered him the complicated secret handshake they'd made up years before. Stanley teared up, then pulled out a handkerchief that turned out to be six feet long. Seb forced a smile.

"Yeah, it's not my best joke," the clown admitted,

honking his nose with the handkerchief. "But we'll miss ya, kid."

Then Seb turned to hug his father, pulling away quickly, aware that if he lingered too long, he'd lose his nerve and never go through with it. "Bye, Dad," he said, and he turned to the attendant who'd come to accompany him.

He began to walk away, then stole a glance back, and the Konstantinov Family Circus waved. Juan turned a backflip. Stanley jingled his shoes.

"*Bon courage!*" called Maxime. "We're counting on you!"

Seb waved back, then turned and hurried away.

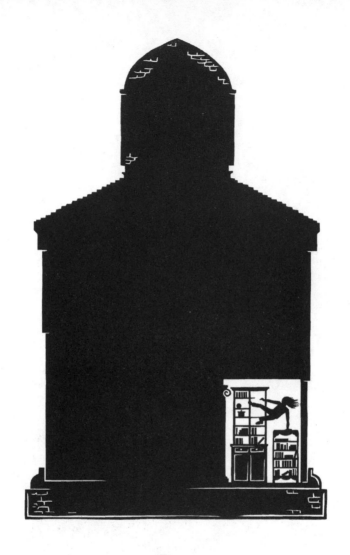

Part 2

THE BONAVENTURE
CIRCUS SCHOOL

SEB STARED OUT the window of the taxi at the dark, rain-slicked streets of Old Montreal and noted that they had passed the same set of streetlights three times. He didn't think this was a good sign.

"What's the name of this school again?" the driver asked over his shoulder.

"Bonaventure," Seb replied.

"Huh." The driver turned back to the road and switched the windshield wipers up to their highest speed. Seb watched them flip back and forth, back and forth, and his eyelids began to droop.

The Scout hadn't been able to pick Seb up at the airport, so he'd sent his regrets with the taxi driver. The man had met him at the baggage claim with a sign that read SEBASTIAN CONSTANTINOPLE. Seb, who had been traveling for over a day thanks to a delayed flight in Frankfurt, decided this was good enough.

"I can't find this place," the driver complained. He spoke English with a French accent, but different than Maxime's, somehow. Seb was too tired to really think about it. "Are you sure it's real?" asked the driver.

Seb shook himself awake. This was something he hadn't considered—that he would arrive in Montreal only to discover that his new school did not, in fact, exist.

Seb peered out the window at Old Montreal. It did look suitably old, with narrow cobblestone streets and the kind of ornate buildings he expected from Europe, but not from Canada. He wondered if there was also a New Montreal, and how it was different, but he decided not to ask, as the driver was growing increasingly grumpy.

"What kind of school is this?" the man huffed as they splashed through a giant puddle.

"A circus school," replied Seb.

"*Quoi?*" The driver stepped on the brakes and looked at Seb wide-eyed through the rearview mirror. "A *circus* school? Like, with acrobats and . . ."—he mimed a three-ball cascade—"*jongleurs?*"

"Jugglers," Seb supplied.

A car behind them honked. The driver made an impolite gesture over his shoulder and started driving again.

"Running away to join the circus," he marveled. "So what do you do?"

"Sorry?"

"Are you a lion tamer? Acrobat? One of those people on the . . ." He waved his hand back and forth in a swinging motion.

"Trapeze?" said Seb.

The driver nodded.

"Uh-uh," Seb replied. "And not all trapezes swing." He leaned forward, resting his elbows on his knees. "The static trapeze barely moves at all. It's more about the shapes the artist makes when they're on it." He paused, thinking about Maria, the Konstantinov aerialist. She'd recently been perfecting a new trapeze trick that involved hanging off it by her neck—no hands or feet involved. He made a mental note to ask how it was going when he called home.

"So if you don't do the trapeze, what do you do?" asked the driver.

Seb drew a breath. He'd spent the better part of the flight from Frankfurt figuring out how he was going to answer this very question. It was part of his big Plan to Survive Circus School. Since he'd had no proper writing paper, he'd written it out on an airplane sick bag. "Well, I'm—"

"Wait, there it is!" The driver pointed left and slammed on the brakes again. "Weird place for a school, but I guess it is the circus, right?" He tapped the meter above his head.

Seb dug out the wad of Canadian bills his father had given him upon leaving Budapest. He had no idea where Dragan had gotten the money—much less Canadian money, much less in Budapest—nor did he particularly want to know. He paid the driver, then they both climbed out into the rain to retrieve his trunk, which fortunately had survived the trip intact.

"*Bonne chance,* kid!" The driver slapped him on the back, then hopped back into the taxi.

"Thanks," Seb said. He grasped the handle of his trunk, shielded his eyes from the rain and looked up for the first time at his new home.

"Wait, what?" He blinked. Before him stood a very large and very old church. A cathedral, actually—with stone spires reaching up into the inky sky. Seb looked back at the taxi driver, who shrugged through the fogged-up window.

"Weird is right," said Seb. He sloshed across the street to the giant wooden double doors, where a plaque declared, in swirling gold script, that he had indeed found the Bonaventure Circus School.

"Okay then," he said. And he squared his shoulders and pulled open the door.

Inside, it took a moment for his eyes to adjust. When they did, he found himself in a dimly lit foyer whose walls and floor were lined with stone. To his left was another set of wooden double doors, which he assumed led into the cathedral. To his right stood an office, locked up tight for the night. And beyond that stretched a narrow stone hallway; the few flickering lights overhead gave no indication where it led. The air was cold and dank.

It felt more like a medieval castle than a circus, Seb decided, setting his trunk down next to his sopping sneakers. "Um, hello?" he called out. "Is anyone here?"

At first he heard nothing but his own voice, bouncing off the stones. But after a few moments, footsteps arose somewhere down the dark hallway. Seb waited, fighting a growing urge to turn and run back out into the rain.

A moment later, a tall, blond man wearing a neat, gray suit walked into the foyer. Or rather, he strode, swinging his arms with the ease of someone who had everything under control. With his broad shoulders and solid jaw, he could have been a strongman in a traditional circus. Or a superhero in a movie.

"Hello." He blinked at Seb. His eyes were steely silver, like Maxime's favorite dagger. "Are you a new student?"

Seb nodded. "I'm Seb."

The man nodded too, but in a way that told Seb he

didn't actually know who he was. "I'm Michel. But around here, they call me the Scout."

So this was the Scout he'd written to. "I'm Sebastian Konstantinov," Seb clarified.

"*Konstantinov!*" The Scout's eyebrows leaped toward his hair, which rivaled Dragan's in terms of thickness and volume. "I'm so sorry! We've been expecting you. I didn't recognize . . . I mean, you look—"

"It's okay," Seb said quickly, knowing exactly what he was about to say: that Seb looked nothing like what he'd expected. In other words, nothing like his father. He reached up to flatten his hair, which even sopping wet still managed to stand on end.

The Scout took Seb's wet hand and shook it hard. "Welcome, Sebastian Konstantinov," he said. "Or Seb, you prefer? I'm very sorry for not meeting you at the airport. We had a bit of an emergency, and I had to stay and take care of it."

"Is everything okay?" asked Seb.

"Oh yes," the Scout assured him. "When your school is this old, things break down all the time. Today it was the stage in the theater—the boards needed patching in time for orientation tomorrow."

"That sounds important," Seb agreed. "So you do carpentry too?"

"I've dabbled in a few different things." The Scout winked at him. "Now, shall I show you your room?" He pointed to Seb's trunk. "Is this all you brought? No other equipment? Unicycles, hula hoops . . ." He scanned the foyer.

"That's it," said Seb.

"Well, then." He picked up the trunk and tucked it under his arm. "This way."

He led Seb down the dark hallway, under the flickering lights. It was eerily quiet; the only sounds came from the Scout's shoes tapping on the stone floor and Seb's sneakers sloshing behind.

It was definitely creepy, Seb decided. But if he'd learned one thing from twelve years in a traveling circus, it was that pretty well everything looked better in daylight. The spooky mountains towering over your caravan might well turn out to be snowcapped and sparkling in the morning. And a little village that looked eerie in the shadows could actually be quite charming.

Hopefully this held true for a circus school in a decrepit old church.

The hallway opened up into a common area, where half a dozen couches clustered around a massive fireplace. To the left was a cafeteria lined with tables, all empty.

"So . . . where is everyone?" Seb asked, trying to sound

casual and not at all concerned. "I thought most students arrive a few days early."

"Only the ones from far away," said the Scout. "Most students live in town or close by, though they still board here throughout the week. They'll arrive first thing tomorrow for orientation. Quiet, isn't it?"

Seb nodded.

"I guess that's the way the monks liked it."

"Monks?"

"Bonaventure used to be a monastery," said the Scout. "Didn't you know?"

A monastery! Seb shook his head. He'd seen several monasteries in his travels, including one in Moldova, where some monks had dug caves into the side of a cliff overlooking a river. He'd sketched that one on his home-made map, which he'd left with Maxime in Budapest.

Like Bonaventure, the cave monastery had been eerily quiet. Though probably, he thought, as he surveyed the stained couches and threadbare carpet, it needed less upkeep.

"The monks left decades ago," the Scout explained. "We now use their dining hall as a cafeteria." He gestured at the empty tables. "And their cathedral as a theater. You'll see that tomorrow at orientation. Some say it's the best part of the school. It's also where we host our Friday night soirees for the circophiles of Montreal."

Circophiles! Seb perked up at the word.

"Students aren't actually invited," the Scout went on, "but perhaps the directrice could make an exception for you someday. The soirees are quite a sight. And they bring in some much-needed money," he added.

It was an odd thing to say to a new student, Seb thought, but there wasn't much point in denying the state of the school. There were holes in the carpet the size of dinner plates.

At the notion of dinner, Seb's stomach growled loudly.

"Ah, of course you're hungry. One moment." The Scout disappeared into the cafeteria, emerging a minute later with an apple and a peanut butter sandwich. "I'm sorry, this is all we've got tonight. Our cook will be back tomorrow morning."

"This is perfect," Seb told him, and he meant it.

"I've never seen a Konstantinov Family Circus show," the Scout said as he led Seb through a door near the cafeteria, then up three flights of stairs. "But I've heard they're excellent."

"They're pretty great," Seb agreed. "Our performers are really talented. I like the sword-swallowing act best, but the contortionist has this great new routine where he fits himself into a guitar case. It's pretty wild." His chest tightened a little. He missed the Konstantinovs already.

The Scout smiled. "Your father has built a real empire over there, hasn't he? I hear he's a visionary."

"A what?" Seb stopped halfway up the second flight of stairs.

"A visionary," the Scout repeated. "Someone with creative and inventive ideas."

Seb knew what a visionary was. He just wasn't sure who would have used the word to describe his father. Except maybe Dragan himself.

He made a polite humming noise and continued climbing.

"We're thrilled to have you here, Seb." The Scout stopped in front of a door marked with the number 5.

"Me too," Seb said, though at that moment, he was more exhausted than anything.

Room Number 5 contained a set of bunk beds, a chest of drawers, a small sink and a carpet as threadbare as the one downstairs. But more important, it contained a boy about Seb's age, who was juggling two oranges and three balled-up socks.

The boy jumped when they entered, and the objects rained down around him. "*Bonsoir!*" he cried.

"*Bonsoir*," Seb replied. "*Je m'appelle Seb.*"

"You speak French!" The Scout looked impressed.

"Our sword swallower is from France," Seb told him, then recalled Dragan's warning. "I mean, my brother—"

"Cool." The boy shook his hand vigorously. "I'm Sylvain."

"Seb," said Seb.

"And your English is very American for someone from Eastern Europe," the Scout observed. "But a few of the Konstantinovs are from America, aren't they? Your performers come from all over the world."

Seb started. "Wait, you know?"

"Know what?" said the Scout.

"Uh, that we're not related?" said Seb. He *told* his father that they'd know!

Both the Scout and Sylvain nodded. "I think I read it on Circopedia," said the Scout.

"I checked out your website," added Sylvain. "You guys look nothing alike."

"Yeah," Seb agreed. It was a relief, actually, to have one less secret to keep from his new classmates and teachers. He had enough to worry about. "So, are you from far away too?" he asked Sylvain.

The boy shook his head. "I'm from Montreal."

"Sylvain decided to come a day early." The Scout chuckled. "To meet his new roommate."

Sylvain didn't deny it. "My friends were pretty jealous when they heard I get to share a room with the superstar," he said.

Seb dropped his sandwich on the carpet. "The what?"

"I took the top bunk," Sylvain went on. "But you can have it if you want. I don't mind."

Seb declined and retrieved his sandwich, though his appetite had disappeared.

"I'll leave you two then," said the Scout. "And I'll see you tomorrow for orientation."

Seb wished him goodnight, then sank down on the bottom bunk, now as perplexed as he was exhausted.

"Hey, you going to eat that?" Sylvain pointed at his apple. Seb shook his head, and Sylvain snatched it up. Then he resumed juggling, this time with three socks, two oranges and one apple.

"So, no offense," the boy said as he tossed the objects in a perfect arc above his head. "But you look different than I imagined. People keep saying you're known for your charisma. So I pictured you, I don't know, taller?" He dropped the socks and began juggling the fruit in one hand.

"*Charisma?*" Seb repeated. It was just getting worse.

"Yeah, you know. Like charm that inspires—"

"I know what it is," he said. What he didn't know was who would call him that. Though he suspected it was the same person who'd called Dragan a visionary.

Now he definitely needed to lie down.

He stretched out on the bottom bunk and closed his eyes, listening to the patter of Sylvain's juggling. It's going to be okay, he told himself. Remember, you've got a Plan to Survive Circus School. He patted the pocket of his jeans, to make sure it was still there, written on the airplane sick bag.

It's going to be okay, he told himself again, and he repeated the words until they became as rhythmic as Sylvain's juggling. Within moments, it lulled him right to sleep.

CONTRARY TO SEB'S theory, Room Number 5 did not look better in the daylight. In fact, the light streaming through its one small window the next morning only illuminated the shabby carpet and the large water stain on the ceiling.

But it wasn't terrible, Seb decided. And since his roommate in the top bunk was still snoring away (not nearly as throatily as Maxime), he took the opportunity to review his Plan to Survive Circus School. He dug into his pocket, as he'd fallen asleep in his clothes, and pulled out the crumpled sick bag to review the plan.

PLAN TO SURVIVE CIRCUS SCHOOL

Option 1: Meet with Angélique Saint-Germain.
Explain that I am a Circus Scholar, here to observe the

ways of the modern circus. As such, I'd be better off
watching during skills classes than participating.

This, he believed, was his best bet. It involved next to no lying and would justify spending most of his time in the library.

Option 2: Fake an injury.

Option two was less desirable. Not only did it involve a pretty big lie, it could land him in a doctor's office. He did, however, have a good injury in mind: the fractured metatarsal. One of the Konstantinov acrobats had once fractured his metatarsal, which was a very important bone in the foot, and he'd been out for weeks.

Option 3: Hide.

He hoped it wouldn't come to option three. That would make for a very long four years. But desperate times called for desperate measures, as they said. And Seb *was* pretty good at blending into the walls.

Soon Sylvain's alarm went off, and the boys rolled out of bed to prepare for the day. For Seb, this involved locating his trunk and digging out some cleaner clothes. For Sylvain, it involved locating a giant bag of candy and digging in.

"That's your breakfast?" Seb was impressed.

"*First* breakfast," Sylvain corrected him. "Second breakfast happens in the cafeteria—toast, cereal, you know." He tossed a handful of gummy bears into his mouth. "Want some?" He held out the bag.

Seb took a string of licorice. "I've never had candy for breakfast," he admitted—although he had, during some particularly lean times for the Konstantinovs, resorted to breakfasting on the previous night's show popcorn. He didn't share this with his roommate.

"Then you've been missing out," Sylvain informed him. "But maybe don't mention my stash. The teachers here want us to eat healthily—they think it improves our performance. But you know what *really* improves performance? Chocolate peanut butter cups." He tossed one in the air and caught it in his teeth. Then he offered one to Seb, who ate it like a normal person.

A knock on the door made them both jump.

"Are you boys ready?" the Scout called from the other side.

"Almost," Sylvain yelled back, hiding his candy bag in the top drawer of the dresser. "Better hurry," he told Seb. "He's taking us to orientation."

"Really?" Seb said. "He does that?"

"Not for everyone." Sylvain pulled on a very wrinkled T-shirt. "Just you, Superstar."

"Oh." Seb's stomach lurched. Clearly there was no time to lose in putting his Plan to Survive Circus School into action. "Hey, do you know where the directrice's office is?" he asked as he changed his clothes.

"Third floor," Sylvain replied. "Why?"

"I want to meet with her," said Seb.

"What?" Sylvain's eyes went wide. "No, you don't."

"Yeah, I do," Seb insisted. "Can't students meet with her?"

"Well sure, they *can*," said Sylvain. "If they're crazy enough to want to. Trust me, you don't—"

"Almost ready?" the Scout called. Seb heard a shout outside the door, followed by laughter.

"Tell you later," Sylvain promised, and he flung open the door.

The Scout stood there waiting, wearing the same spotless suit as the night before. His hair was once again perfectly coiffed, and Seb wondered if he slathered it in hot oil at bedtime to make it shiny, or if that was just a Dragan thing.

He stepped into the hallway to find a completely different scene than the night before. Now the old carpet was strewn with duffel bags and suitcases, juggling pins and unicycles. And there were kids everywhere—mostly boys, as this was the boys' wing—laughing and chattering away.

"Ready for breakfast?" the Scout asked. "You must be hungry."

"Not really." Sylvain bounced out to greet a few boys with high fives. The boys, however, seemed more interested in Seb; several stared at him openly. He even caught one mouthing, "It's the superstar!"

"Not really," Seb agreed. On the contrary, he once again felt a little ill.

"Well, then, I'll show you around some more," the Scout said. "Follow me." He sidestepped a hula hoop and led Seb down the hall. Sylvain followed close behind.

"It's him!" one boy said to another as they passed.

"Really? *That's* him?" his friend whispered back.

Seb blushed to the roots of his hair.

"Move along, kids!" Sylvain commanded. "Nothing to see here. Give my roommate some space!" He nudged the boys aside so Seb could pass.

"But it *is* him, right?" one of the boys asked Sylvain.

"Of course it's him. And he has a name," Sylvain replied haughtily. "It's Sebastian Konstantinov. Did I mention he's my roommate?"

Never had Seb wanted so badly to blend into the walls.

"There are sixty students at Bonaventure this year," the Scout said as they left the boys' wing. "About fifteen in each year. We have all disciplines represented, from acrobatics to unicycling."

Seb tried to ignore the stares and hurried to catch up. "Where have they all trained?" he asked.

"Theaters, dance schools, gymnastics clubs," the Scout replied. "Some, like Sylvain, trained at smaller circus schools. And there are always a few with no formal training at all, who simply show tremendous talent. My favorite part of my job," he added, "is finding those students—the ones who've never before even considered studying circus arts."

"Where do you find them?" Seb asked.

"You never know where they'll be." The Scout grinned. "I like to think I have a sixth sense for it."

Before Seb could ask more questions, the Scout led him into the girls' wing, which looked identical to the one they'd left, except now all the kids shouting and laughing were female. Two girls sporting matching purple T-shirts and pixie-like haircuts appeared to be practicing an acrobatics routine in the middle of the hallway, despite the bags and suitcases around them.

"Look out," Sylvain warned as they began to cartwheel toward them. Seb jumped out of the way, only to land right on someone's foot.

"Ow!" the someone cried out.

"Sorry!" Seb whirled around to find a very tall girl scowling down at him. Her face was long and thin, her brown eyes so dark they were nearly black. She wore boys' shorts and sneakers, and her hair reminded Seb of the Konstantinov lion's mane, except dark like her eyes.

"Sorry," he said again. "I was just trying to avoid them." He gestured to the twin pixies, who were now walking down the hall on their hands.

"Join the club," the girl said darkly. "And be glad they're not your roommates."

"This is Francesca de Luca," said the Scout. "She's one of those rare talents I just mentioned. Francesca—"

"Frankie," the girl cut in.

"Frankie," said the Scout, "has no formal circus training, but she is a brilliant, self-taught freerunner."

"*Traceur,*" Frankie corrected him. "I do parkour."

"Cool!" Sylvain held up his hand for a high five. Frankie regarded it for a moment, then left him hanging. Sylvain shrugged and high-fived himself with his other hand.

Seb had seen some kids in Prague practicing parkour, so he knew it involved using the city as an obstacle course. He recalled them scaling walls and flipping off ledges, and feeling certain that if he attempted it, he'd end up in a full-body cast.

"I discovered Frankie in Rome," the Scout said. "It was a stroke of luck, really. Frankie, this is Sebastian Konstantinov, of the Konstantinov Family Circus."

Frankie looked him up and down. "Never heard of it."

The Scout started. Sylvain snorted. But Seb was only relieved: at least one person at Bonaventure didn't think he was a superstar.

Before the Scout could explain, Frankie excused herself to go unpack.

They continued on, down three flights of stairs and a few dark hallways until they reached the front foyer where Seb had stood the previous night.

"This way." The Scout led them to the other set of wooden double doors and pushed them open. "This is the Bonaventure theater."

Seb stepped inside and froze. "Whoa," he breathed.

It was, as the Scout had said, a cathedral—or had been, at one time. Parts of the original church remained, like cream-colored marble arches and statues of dour-looking saints. Overhead, stained glass windows beamed rainbow light onto the wooden floors. But the church pews had been removed, replaced by rows of folding chairs. The rafters were rigged with bolts and hooks for the trapeze and silks. And where the altar once stood there was now a big stage.

"This is amazing!" Seb whispered, imagining the shows that could take place here, under the stained glass windows and sky-high ceilings. It would be beautiful and haunting and just . . . just . . .

"Perfect," he breathed.

"Far from it," sighed the Scout. "This place needs a lot of work. Ideally, we'd rebuild the theater altogether, but that costs a lot of money."

On closer inspection, Seb could see what he meant. The floors were hopelessly scratched and the purple stage curtain stained. The stage bowed dangerously in the middle, and it had clearly been patched several times over the years.

And yet, he still loved everything about the theater. In fact, the only thing he'd change would be to have the place all to himself. Students had begun to stream in around them, claiming seats for orientation. There was a clamor onstage too, where a bald man in a suit was scurrying around, giving orders to some stagehands.

Somewhere backstage, a woman hollered, "Bruno!" The bald man jumped and ducked behind the curtain.

"Come this way." The Scout led the boys up to the very front row.

Seb hesitated—front and center was Dragan's preferred spot, not his. He glanced behind and saw Frankie de Luca claiming the very best seat, in the back corner. He wished he could join her, though she did scare him a little. Maybe more than a little.

As if she could hear his thoughts, Frankie looked over and gazed back at him coolly. He quickly looked away.

And that was when he first saw the staircase.

It stood at the back of the theater, its crooked steps winding up to what looked like a large wooden box with no lid. At one time, Seb guessed, it might have been a choir box for the monks; now it looked largely unused, judging by the rope that cordoned it off.

Sylvain poked him in the ribs, and he turned to find his roommate surrounded by other students. Seb recognized the twin pixies from the girls' floor, plus a few boys who'd sized him up earlier.

"This is my roommate, Sebastian Konstantinov. But you can call him Seb," Sylvain informed them. "We all know each other from circus classes around here," he told Seb. Then he rattled off a list of names, most of which Seb promptly forgot.

"Did you hear that Madeleine didn't get in?" one of the pixies asked. The twins' names were Camille and Giselle, but Seb couldn't for the life of him remember which was which. "Apparently, she's on the wait list."

"Apparently, there are *fifty* kids on the wait list," the other pixie added. Seb decided to call her Giselle.

"It's always like that," Sylvain said wisely. "And a few always get in late. Because someone always gets kicked out."

"They do?" said Seb. He didn't like the sound of that.

"That's what I've heard too," said one of the boys,

a juggler named Matthieu.

"Well, it won't be us," Camille said to Giselle. "Swear it." She held up her pinkie, and her twin hooked her own around it to swear.

"Just don't get on *her* bad side." Sylvain leaned in and lowered his voice. "I've heard awful stories of what happens when kids end up in her office."

Before Seb could ask him to explain, the lights flickered and dimmed, then went off completely. The students and staff fell silent, waiting in the dark.

For a few moments, nothing happened. Then, suddenly, a spotlight flared and the curtains were swept aside to reveal a small woman clad completely in crimson, from her high heels to her suit to her short crimson-colored hair. Or was it scarlet? Seb wondered, and he wished that Juan the contortionist were there to weigh in.

The woman marched across the stage toward a microphone, and the audience burst into applause. She acknowledged it with a nod, and the students cheered.

This, Seb decided, could be none other than Angélique Saint-Germain.

"It's her!" Camille squealed.

"She's just as beautiful in real life as in the photos in her biography," whispered Giselle.

"*Destined to Soar*," added Camille.

Sylvain snorted.

Angélique Saint-Germain *was* beautiful, just as Dragan had said. If Seb hadn't known she was his father's age, he would have assumed her much younger. Possibly she too spent a lot of time on her pores.

Madame Saint-Germain reached the microphone and gestured for silence. The students immediately fell so quiet that Seb could hear the twin pixies breathing, in perfect unison of course. "Welcome," said the directrice, "to a brand-new year at the Bonaventure Circus School."

"Thank you," Camille whispered reverently.

"Would you stop?" Sylvain hissed at her.

"As you know, Bonaventure has extremely high standards," the directrice told them. "You have all been accepted or invited to continue based on your talent and potential for greatness. It was a rigorous audition process, and many did not survive it." She paused, as if taking a moment of silence for the fallen. Seb couldn't help but picture them hidden away somewhere, like in a pit beneath the stage.

"And you might be thinking that now the hardest part is over." The directrice smiled at them, then shook her head. "You would be wrong."

The room grew even quieter.

"As you returning students know, a school year at Bonaventure is challenging. Arduous," she added, rolling her Rs with gusto. "*Grueling*, even. You must balance skills training with excellence in academia. I'll be honest with you," she said, lowering her voice. "Some of you will fail. And there is a long list of students waiting to take your place."

"This is some pep talk," Sylvain whispered.

Seb stole a quick glance at his fellow students, all of whom had survived the grueling audition process that he surely would have failed. He took a deep breath to quell the panic rising in his chest.

You've got a survival plan, he reminded himself. Though now he was seriously questioning the part that required him to meet face-to-face with this crimson-clad woman. She was even more frightening than Frankie de Luca.

"So how does a student succeed at Bonaventure?" the directrice went on.

Camille's hand shot up in the air.

"The answer," the directrice went on, ignoring her, "is, diligence. Dedication. *Devotion*, even."

"That's what I was going to say," Camille whispered.

Sylvain rolled his eyes to the rafters.

"You must pursue perfection, practice at every opportunity," said the directrice. "You are here because you want to be world-class circus performers. And that does not happen without thousands upon thousands of hours of work."

"Sounds exhausting." Sylvain's friend Matthieu yawned.

"It will be," Camille said. She turned to her twin. "But we'll practice 'til we drop, won't we? We'll give up sleeping if we have to." Giselle nodded, though a little reluctantly, and they pinkie swore again. Seb wondered how Frankie would survive the year with the twins as roommates.

"If you fail to practice, you may be asked to leave Bonaventure," said the directrice. "But there are other ways to fail, of course." She began to count them on her crimson fingernails. "Not excelling academically. Not perfecting all your skills. Not respecting teachers. Not arriving on—"

A clamor at the back of the theater interrupted her. Seb turned around. Near the doors huddled a group of adults—teachers, Seb assumed—whispering amongst themselves. The directrice cleared her throat into the microphone, but they didn't seem to hear.

"Am I interrupting something?" Angélique Saint-Germain called out, as if the teachers were misbehaving students.

"*Non, Madame!*" The bald man who'd been onstage earlier popped out of the huddle and trotted down the aisle toward her, a slip of paper in hand. She snatched it from him, scanned it, then quietly cursed. Or rather, it would have been quiet had she not still been holding the microphone.

Some students gasped. A few more giggled.

The directrice cleared her throat. "It appears," she said, "one of the first-year students has gone missing."

"Missing!" The students buzzed.

"A student"—she checked the paper—"named Banjo Brady."

"Banjo?" Sylvain exclaimed. "That's a name?"

Angélique Saint-Germain glared down at him, and he snapped his mouth shut. Then she raised an eyebrow at the bald man.

"That's his name," the man confirmed.

She handed the paper back. "If anyone has seen Monsieur Brady today, please report to the teachers at the back of the room immediately."

A few students hopped up and hurried down the aisle, and the room began to buzz again.

"Maybe he ran away," said Matthieu.

"I bet he couldn't take the pressure," said Camille.

"But what if he got kidnapped!" squeaked Giselle.

"Doubtful," Sylvain said. "He probably just lost his way. Or fell through a hole in the floorboards. I almost did this morning. Anyway"—he shrugged—"when Bingo gets back—"

"I think it's Banjo," said Seb.

"When Banjo gets back," Sylvain went on, "he'll end up in her office for sure." He nodded at the directrice. "And

I've heard that some students who go in . . ." he lowered his voice to a whisper, "never come back out!"

"That's not true!" cried Giselle.

"That's the rumor." Sylvain shrugged. "Maybe it's not true, but I'm not taking chances."

Seb shivered. He could only hope it wasn't true. For Banjo Brady's sake, of course, but especially for his own.

AN HOUR LATER, sixty students spilled out of the Bonaventure theater, sweeping Seb along with them. His arms were full of papers and his brain full of teacher names and dorm rules and the many ways to get kicked out of circus school. The directrice had eventually run out of fingers on which to count them.

The students scattered, heading off to class, but Seb hung back. He needed to find the Scout.

He found the man striding down the dark stone hallway toward the front door, clearly on a mission.

"Mr. Scout!" Seb called, trotting after him. "Can you hang on a minute?"

The Scout turned. "Ah, Seb," he said. "I'm sorry I left without you. I've got to go search for the lost boy, Banjo Brady."

Seb pictured him trading his spotless suit for a superhero costume, then bursting out onto the mean streets of Montreal to fight off the baddies who'd captured poor Banjo Brady. It would make a great story; he made a mental note to come back to it later.

"Right," he said. "I just need to know how I can, um, get a meeting . . . with the directrice."

The Scout looked concerned. "Is something wrong, Seb?"

"Oh, no," Seb said quickly. "I just . . ." He thought fast. "My dad actually asked me to meet with her. To, um, pass on a friendly hello." He hated lying, especially to the Scout. But he told himself it was for a good cause.

The man's face relaxed. "Of course," he said. "I'm sure she'd be delighted. I'll talk to Bruno, her assistant, and set something up. Now, what's your first class?"

"Um . . ." Seb rifled through his papers for his schedule. "Basic Acrobatics," he said, and he cringed, recalling the last time he'd attempted acrobatics. The three Konstantinov acrobats had unanimously agreed that he should never try it again.

"I'll take you there," said the Scout. "Your instructor is Monsieur Gerard, and he likes students to be punctual."

The Scout marched him over to the gymnasium, where the first years were gathered, already dressed in their gym clothes. All thirteen of them turned to stare when Seb slipped in.

Monsieur Gerard, a small, slender man with a pencil-thin mustache, glanced at the clock on the wall, then back at Seb. His mustache twitched.

"Sorry we're late," said the Scout. "This is Sebastian Konstantinov." He leaned over. "I'll leave you now," he whispered to Seb. "Good luck." And he disappeared back out the door, off to save the missing boy from whatever fate had befallen him.

"Ah, *Konstantinov*." Monsieur Gerard's face didn't exactly soften, but his mustache stopped twitching. "Welcome. We're just getting started. Change your clothes and meet us back here."

Seb did as he was told, rejoining the class in his shorts and sneakers.

"The name 'Basic Acrobatics' is misleading," Monsieur Gerard was explaining. "It sounds very simple, and for some it might be second nature."

Camille and Giselle exchanged smiles and nods.

"But it is one of the most important classes you will attend this year. Here we will perfect our form and balance and flexibility—essential qualities for all other skills classes you take. Like our directrice so eloquently put it this morning . . ." He closed his eyes as if replaying her speech. "We will devote ourselves to the pursuit of perfection, to mastering the minute."

Matthieu yawned.

"We have much to cover and no time to lose," Monsieur Gerard said, opening his eyes. "We'll stretch as we introduce ourselves."

While they limbered up their shoulders and hamstrings and wrists, each student took a turn introducing themselves and describing their training. As the Scout had said, nearly everyone had taken dance or gymnastics or circus lessons—some practically since they could walk. The exception was Frankie de Luca, the self-taught *traceur*.

This wasn't the only thing that set Frankie apart. She was nearly a head taller than most students, and still dressed in boys' shorts and a T-shirt instead of a leotard and tights like most other girls. Her hair was knotted atop her head in what reminded Seb of a rat's nest he once found in Dragan's costume closet.

"Sebastian Konstantinov," said Monsieur Gerard. "You hardly need an introduction, but please, tell us about yourself."

Seb cleared his throat and readied himself for the first test of his Plan to Survive Circus School. "Okay. Well, I'm Seb. I grew up in a traditional traveling circus, so I came here to study the modern circus. I'm not an acrobat," he added. "I'm . . . I'm more of a circus scholar."

"A circus scholar." Monsieur Gerard stared at him for a moment, smoothing the hairs in his mustache, which all appeared to be precisely the same length. "I . . . see. Well, I think you're being too humble. You can't have grown up in a circus and not mastered many skills. I'm sure we'll all learn from you."

"Oh, no, I—" Seb began to protest, but Monsieur Gerard had already turned to the next student, a stocky boy with forearms the size of a grown man's.

"I'm Murray," the boy declared. "I've been studying the trapeze for five years already. I'm basically a master."

"But he's really known for his humility," Sylvain added under his breath.

Monsieur Gerard's mustache twitched again, but he only nodded, then turned to the twin pixies, who declared in unison that they'd been practicing acrobatics together since age four. Then came the jugglers, Sylvain and Matthieu, followed by three girls who'd trained on the silks and the aerial hoop, two trampolinists, a boy who did acrobatics on horseback, and a brother and sister unicycle duo.

"Now then," the teacher said once introductions were over. "Let's begin with some simple tumbling." He gestured for them all to sit down. "Wait, Sebastian. Not you."

Seb froze halfway to the floor. "Sorry?"

"You will demonstrate for us. Just a few simple somersaults, forward and back," Monsieur Gerard added, as if it was the easiest thing in the world. As if Seb did somersaults in his sleep.

"Oh, um." Seb swallowed, recalling the Konstantinov acrobats' unanimous advice. "I'd really rather watch, if that's okay."

Monsieur Gerard looked surprised.

"I mean, I have so much to learn about modern performances," Seb hurried on. "The Konstantinov Family Circus is so traditional and . . . outdated. Backward, really," he added, with silent apologies to his family.

"Nonsense," said Monsieur Gerard. "Tumbling is tumbling. Come on now, let's not waste time."

Seb straightened slowly, trying to stay calm and remember his survival plan. His first excuse clearly wasn't working. Was it time to try the fractured metatarsal? Was it too late to hide?

But before he could decide, the gymnasium door swung open and the Scout strode in. He stopped and glanced behind him, then beckoned with a finger. A moment later, a small boy shuffled in. He had blond hair that fell past his shoulders, and he wore a hooded sweatshirt and grass-stained jeans.

"Everyone, this is Banjo Brady," the Scout announced,

placing a hand on the boy's shoulder.

The class gasped.

"Safe and sound." The Scout patted Banjo on the head, and the boy managed a weak smile.

"Banjo Brady!" Monsieur Gerard looked from the boy to the Scout, and the Scout returned a look that said, "I'll explain later." The teacher cleared his throat. "Well. Join us, Banjo. But change your clothes first." He looked at Banjo's jeans, and his mustache twitched again.

Banjo trotted off to the change rooms, and the Scout strode back out, off on his next mission. Seb wished he'd take him along.

Monsieur Gerard sighed impatiently. "Where were we? Ah yes, tumbling. I need someone to demonstrate. There's no time to—"

Camille's and Giselle's hands shot up. "We'll do it!"

Seb stood very still and pretended to be invisible.

"Fine, fine." Monsieur Gerard waved at them. "But only one of you!"

While the girls played a hasty game of rock-paper-scissors to determine who would demonstrate, Seb sat down, relieved. He'd escaped this time, but just barely.

He could only hope the Scout was marching off to book Seb's meeting with the directrice. He clearly couldn't wait much longer.

★ ★ ★

BUT WHEN BASIC ACROBATICS ended an hour later, Seb still hadn't received word from the directrice. He checked his schedule, hoping for mathematics or recess—anything but another circus skills class.

The schedule read "Introduction to Clowning." Seb tried not to groan.

The good news was that the clown teacher, Audrey Petit, was nothing like Monsieur Gerard. For one thing, she smiled—a lot. And she wore rainbow-print pants that billowed when she walked—or more precisely, pranced—around the room. She didn't have a clock in her classroom, and only welcomed Banjo Brady when he wandered in late, still looking lost. What's more, she insisted the students call her by her first name.

"Unless, of course, I'm in clown mode," she added with a big smile. "In which case, my name is Audacité!"

This made most students giggle, but Seb understood. All clowns had two personalities: there was the everyday person, who wore normal-sized shoes and had a normal job—say, in nursing or insurance. And then there was the inner clown, who emerged when the everyday person slipped on a big red nose or a wig or a mask. The inner clown was like the everyday person, but with bigger emotions and reactions. They never tried to hide their feelings.

Seb had always loved to watch the Konstantinov clown slip into clown mode—from a distance, of course, so as not to disturb him. Stanley would simply put on his clown nose and giant red shoes, and just like that, the tax accountant from New Jersey would become Snickertoot the clown.

Back when the Konstantinovs still held out hope for Seb as a performer, he'd had to take lessons from Snickertoot. For two weeks, he'd practiced falling down, bursting spontaneously into tears and imitating random people on the street. And at the end of this trial period, Snickertoot had come to an important conclusion.

"You're not funny, kid," he'd said.

"Really?" Seb had sighed, though he wasn't surprised.

"Not that all clowns are," the clown went on. "There are plenty of sad clowns in the world. But I don't think you're one of those either." He studied Seb for a moment, then whipped a water pistol out of his jacket pocket and squirted him between the eyes.

Seb sputtered and wiped his face with his sleeve.

"See?" Snickertoot shook his head. "You're just not entertaining. Better try something else."

Seb remembered that advice now, as Audrey Petit pranced around the room, handing each student a spongy red nose.

"I'm sure you're well acquainted with these," she whispered as she pressed one into Seb's hand. "I know we can all learn from your expertise!"

"Oh, I'm not a clown," he told her. "I'm actually a circus schol—" But she moved on before he could explain.

He glanced around at his fellow first-years. Camille and Giselle were comparing noses to make sure theirs were identical, while Sylvain was balancing his on his real nose like a seal. Frankie, once again, looked less than thrilled, but this might have been because she was stuck sitting beside Murray, the trapeze "master." He seemed to be telling her all about his training. She seemed to not care a bit.

"The nose is a very important part of clowning," Audrey told them once everyone had received theirs. "Once you put it on, you're no longer yourself." She held up her own red ball and popped it on her face. "See? Now I'm Audacité!"

She gestured for everyone to put their noses on. Seb did so reluctantly, with silent apologies to Snickertoot for not heeding his advice.

Audacité beamed at him. "This must be second nature for you, Seb."

"It really isn't," he insisted. "I'm not a clown."

"Yeah, the superstar's a *circus scholar*," Murray piped up.

A few kids gasped. All heads whipped toward Murray, then over to Seb.

"What?" Murray said innocently. "That's what he said, isn't it?"

Seb felt his face turn scarlet, or maybe crimson. He glared at Murray, then turned to Audacité to explain. "My circus back home is really traditional and outdated. So I came here to watch and study the modern circus."

Audrey slipped off her nose and smiled down at him. "As I'm sure you know, clowning is a very old art," she said. "And traditional clowns are very much like modern clowns. I think you know a lot about clowning, Seb. And I know we're all going to learn from you." She winked at him.

"No, but—"

"You just haven't discovered your inner clown yet," she went on. "There's one inside each of us, and this year, we're going to uncover them!" She spun around, rainbow pants billowing.

"It will be an incredible journey," she went on. "When you get to know your inner clown, you get to know the person you really are deep inside, not just the person you might sometimes pretend to be. It can be soul-expanding!"

Seb stole another glance at Frankie, who now looked a little nauseated. But again, this might have been because of Murray. He was whispering to her, but loud enough that everyone could hear.

"I just don't buy that you're self-taught," he said. "Come clean—where'd you train?"

Frankie rolled her eyes but didn't reply.

"You've got a secret, don't you?" he persisted.

"Murray, be quiet," Sylvain told him.

"Clowns love new experiences," Audrey went on, ignoring Murray's bad manners. "They're always willing to say yes. So with that in mind, we're going to play a game. This one is called 'Yes, Let's!'"

A game already? Once again, Seb swallowed a groan.

"Everyone will start by finding a partner," said Audrey. "Seb? Would you help me demonstrate?"

"Me?" Seb couldn't believe it. *Again?*

"It's easy, I promise," said Audrey. "All you have to do is say yes. One person will suggest an activity, and their partner will agree to it, with a resounding 'Yes, Let's!' Then you'll go off and do it."

It did sound easy, but still Seb resisted, recalling Snickertoot's advice. Meanwhile, Murray kept on pestering Frankie, his voice growing louder.

"I bet you're, like, Italian royalty," he said.

"Italy's a democracy," Frankie informed him. "And you're an idiot."

Murray was undeterred. "Or maybe a member of the Mafia!"

"Murray stop!" Camille shushed him. But now all the students were listening to him instead of their teacher. It did seem likely that Frankie the self-taught *traceur* had an interesting past. But Seb was pretty sure this wasn't the way to uncover it.

"I know—you're a criminal!" Murray declared. "Covering up a life of crime!"

"Now pay attention, everyone." Audrey clapped her hands. "Seb, you'll help demonstrate, won't you?"

Seb turned back to the teacher, once again wishing he'd talked to the directrice before classes began. But before he could explain the circus scholar thing once again, a loud noise across the room made everyone turn.

It was a vaguely familiar noise. It sounded a bit like the Konstantinov lion when she got really sick of having her picture taken.

Except the Konstantinov lion didn't swear in Italian.

Seb turned around just in time to see Frankie wind up and punch Murray in the nose.

9

A T LUNCHTIME, it was all anyone could talk about.
"Did you hear the *crunch*?"
"I'll never forget it!"
"Did you see the blood?"
"It was a gusher."
"Did Camille really pass out?"
"Giselle had to drag her to the nurse's office."

Seb couldn't blame them—it was an excellent story. And Murray wasn't badly hurt; his nose wasn't even broken, though it would have to be bandaged for a few weeks.

But as the lunch hour wore on, Seb grew tired of hearing the story retold, and his mind began to wander. It was evening in Eastern Europe, so the Konstantinovs were likely preparing for a show, possibly trying to round up some locals with popcorn bribes. His chest tightened so painfully at the thought that he had to put down his half-eaten ham sandwich.

"You okay?" asked Sylvain, who was now on his third sandwich. "You're looking a little . . ." He closed his eyes and stuck out his tongue.

"I think it's jet lag," Seb said. It wasn't true, but Sylvain accepted it. He turned back to his friends to debate exactly how much blood had poured out of Murray's nose that morning.

To distract himself, both from the debate and from thoughts of home, Seb returned to the story he'd been tossing around for weeks: the Konstantinov animals' daring escape from the Bucharest Zoo. Each time he thought about it, he added a few more details or a new plot twist. Most recently, he'd decided that the monkey would find an old tarp and drape it over the elephant, so that when they encountered humans, everyone could hide underneath it and pretend to be a tent. It was pretty ingenious.

"Have you seen her, Seb?"

"Sorry, what?" Seb dragged himself back to the cafeteria.

"Frankie," said Matthieu. "Have you seen her since . . ." He mimed a left hook and made a crunching noise.

"Nope," said Seb.

Sylvain shook his head. "She must have been sent to

the directrice's office. That's two first-years on the first day!"

"Do you think that's a record?" asked Matthieu. They began to debate.

Seb tuned them out again, wishing he could be by himself to think. But where would one go to think at Bonaventure? There were kids everywhere.

Suddenly, he remembered the choir box in the theater. It would make the perfect thinking spot—devoid of students and quiet as, well, a church.

Could he sneak in and use it? he wondered. Could he go *now*?

As if in reply, the bell rang, signaling an end to lunch.

"What's next?" asked Sylvain.

Seb pulled out his schedule, praying it wouldn't be juggling.

"English," he said, brightening.

Sylvain groaned. "My worst subject. I was hoping for juggling."

Seb kept his thoughts to himself.

FROM THE MOMENT Seb laid eyes on Oliver Grey, he knew they were going to get along just fine. First of all, the English teacher wasn't a circus performer—that much was obvious from his rather rotund frame. He wore spectacles and old green sneakers, and he had a bushy red beard flecked with what appeared to be bits of ham sandwich. And like Audrey, he told the students to call him by his first name.

But the best thing about Oliver was that during their first class of the year, he took the students to the library.

"Go nuts in here, guys," Oliver said as they filed inside. "Nuts in a respectful, library-voice kind of way," he added when the librarian gave him a dirty look. "Bonaventure has an amazing collection of circus books."

The library was a cavernous room, low on light like much of the school. It smelled a bit mildewy and definitely needed a good dusting, but none of that bothered Seb, for the library had more books than he'd ever seen. The shelves bowed under their weight, and many were stacked in tall piles on the floor, like stalagmites in a cave.

Seb hurried to the farthest corner of the room and began to inspect the collection. There were books on circus history and circus theory. There were books on circuses around the world, from Australia to Zimbabwe. There were books on juggling and trapeze rigging and unicycle maintenance—and even one old, worn hardcover called, curiously, *L'art du pickpocket*. And to Seb's delight, there was also a small section of novels.

He chose one titled *Escape from the Haunted Prison* and sank down on the floor to dig in. But no sooner had he opened it than he noticed a pair of green sneakers stop in front of him.

"Oh, hi." Seb looked up at Oliver Grey. "Am I allowed to read this?" He held up his book. "I know it isn't about the circus, but it looks pretty good."

"Of course," said Oliver. "It's a great story. But, um, Seb . . ." He crouched down beside him.

"What's wrong?" Seb asked, and for a moment he panicked, assuming bad news from back home. An aerial hoop accident, maybe, or an incorrectly swallowed cutlass.

"You've been called to the directrice's office," said Oliver.

"Oh!" Seb slammed his book shut. "Finally!" He hopped up and dusted off his pants. "Where is it?"

Oliver stood up slowly, still looking concerned. "Third floor. Turn right outside the stairway. It's two doors down on the left. But Seb . . ." He tugged on his beard, releasing some bits of ham. "I don't want to scare you, but this usually isn't a good thing."

"Oh, it's okay," Seb assured him. "I requested it."

"You did?"

Seb nodded. "Can you keep this book for me? I'd like to sign it out."

Oliver took the book. "Sure, no problem. But . . ." He looked left and right, then lowered his voice. "A word of advice, Seb: agree with everything she says. No matter what."

"I will," Seb promised. Then he turned and jogged out of the library.

He found the directrice's office right where Oliver said it would be. A plaque on the door read ANGÉLIQUE SAINT-GERMAIN, DIRECTRICE in swirling gold script.

He squared his shoulders. Even if she was a little scary, this visit would be worth it. Everything would get easier once it was over. Maybe she would give him a note to present to teachers—like a doctor's note, excusing him from attempting all circus skills. Maybe she still had some of that nice heavy paper, smooth to the touch.

He let himself into her office.

The first thing he saw was the bald man from orientation. He was seated at a desk that was far too small for him—so small, in fact, that it looked like it belonged to a child. A sign atop it told Seb he was BRUNO LAMBERT, ASSISTANT À LA DIRECTRICE.

The second thing he saw was a bench against the wall, upon which sat none other than Banjo Brady and Frankie de Luca.

"Um, hi," Seb said to Bruno, who was typing away on his computer, which barely fit on the desk. "I have an appointment with the directrice."

"She's on a call," Bruno said without looking up. "Take a seat with the other bêtes noires."

"Oh!" Seb was startled, partly because it was rude; a bête noire was a dislikeable person—a beast. Also, Bruno was lumping him in with Banjo and Frankie, and he hadn't caused any trouble.

"I actually requested this meeting," Seb told him, just to clarify. But Bruno was still typing intently at his tiny desk, like a pianist pounding a concerto on a miniature piano. So Seb did as he'd been told and joined the bêtes noires on the bench.

"Hello," Banjo said softly when he sat down.

"Hi," said Seb. He nodded at Frankie, and she nodded back. Then they all sat in silence, waiting for the directrice to get off the phone.

After a few minutes, Frankie turned to Seb. "So what are you in for?" she asked.

Again, he was startled. "Sorry, what?"

"What you're in for," Frankie repeated. "You know. I'm here because I clocked the trapeze master this morning." She shrugged, not looking terribly remorseful.

"And I'm here because I went missing," said Banjo.

"Right." Seb looked at him. "So what happened to you?"

"I just went outside," Banjo said simply. "See, when the Scout first discovered me, at Logger Sports Day—"

"Hang on." Frankie held up a hand. "Logger Sports Day?"

Banjo nodded. "Don't you have that where you're from?"

Frankie and Seb shook their heads.

"Oh, that's too bad." Banjo looked genuinely sad for them. "It's a tradition in Stumpville—that's the town I'm from, on the West Coast. On Logger Sports Day, we have competitions like tree climbing, ax throwing and tree felling. That kind of thing."

"Wow." Seb tried to picture it, but it sounded like nothing he'd ever experienced. "And the Scout just . . . showed up? In Stumpville?"

Banjo nodded. "It was a little surprising."

"I'll say," Seb said, recalling how the Scout had called his ability to find circus talent a "sixth sense."

"Were you competing at . . . Logger Sports Day?" Frankie asked. She sounded like she still didn't believe it was a thing.

Banjo nodded. "I was slacklining. That's like tightrope walking, but on a loose rope close to the ground. I also highline—that's the same thing, but high above the ground. And I trickline, which means I throw in some tricks now and then. It's pretty fun."

Seb nodded, though it sounded to him like a direct route to the emergency room. "So back to this morning . . ."

"Right, so when I met the Scout, he told me that Montreal would be nothing like Stumpville, which is all mountains and rainforests, but that somewhere in the middle of the city, there's a big forest on a mountain. I thought maybe I could visit it before orientation started."

"So you just went by yourself?" Seb asked, incredulous. "Do you know Montreal at all?"

"No," Banjo said. "But I don't usually get lost. I have what Lily calls an internal compass."

"Lily?" said Frankie.

"Internal compass?" said Seb.

"Lily's my mom," Banjo explained. "My parents like me to call them by their first names, kind of like our clown teacher. Theo and Lily aren't into traditional hierarchical structures."

"I see," said Seb, though he didn't really. Frankie raised an eyebrow.

"And an internal compass keeps you from getting lost," Banjo went on. "At least it did back home. Anyway, I didn't know that we're not allowed outside by ourselves without permission here. I've never had to ask permission." He sighed.

"Huh." Frankie considered his story for a moment, then turned back to Seb. "You didn't answer me. What are you in for?"

"Nothing, actually," Seb told her. "I asked to meet with the directrice."

"You *what?*" she exclaimed.

"Are you sure you want to do that?" Banjo's eyes were wide.

The phone on Bruno's desk rang, and he picked it up. "*Oui, Madame,*" he said, then set it back down. "She's ready for you," he said.

"Which one of us?" asked Frankie.

"You," Bruno pointed at Seb.

"Oh, but . . ." Seb looked at Frankie and Banjo. "They've been here longer than—"

"You're first," Bruno told him. "And trust me, you don't want to keep her waiting."

10

U PON ENTERING Angélique Saint-Germain's office, Seb had to pause to let his eyes adjust to the low light. What was it with Bonaventure and shoddy lightbulbs? he wondered. Dragan would have been horrified. In the Konstantinov Family Circus, there was always enough money for the kind of bulbs that nicely illuminated one's pores, even if it meant the performers had to breakfast on stale popcorn now and then.

Something growled at Seb's feet.

"Oh!" He jumped at the sight of a large, brown bulldog. "Hi, there." He crouched and offered the dog his hand to smell, but it only heaved itself up off the floor and stomped off.

Seb watched it trudge across the room to an enormous desk, behind which sat Angélique Saint-Germain.

"Oh!" Seb jumped again. "Hi! I didn't see you there. Sorry."

"Sebastian Konstantinov," said the directrice. "Do come in and sit down."

Her deep, clear voice sounded welcoming enough, but Seb hurried over all the same, taking in the room as he crossed it. On one wall, a massive picture window looked down on the school gymnasium, in which three older students were currently wheeling around on one unicycle. This meant the directrice could watch classes from above—Seb made a mental note of it.

He hustled on, past a grand piano that, judging by the layer of dust on it, hadn't been played in years. An ivory bust atop it looked suspiciously like the directrice, but Seb didn't stop to inspect it. He didn't want to keep her waiting.

Her desk was a marvel in itself, made of rich, red wood and roughly the size of a small whale. Angélique Saint-Germain looked even more petite than usual seated behind it on what looked like a throne lined with purple velvet.

"Sit, please." She gestured to a small metal stool opposite the desk. Seb did as he was told, and she took a moment to look him over, from the tips of his hurricane hair to the toes of his sneakers. He thought he saw the corners of her mouth droop, but she smoothed it into a smile.

"Well," she said. "Here you are. You've arrived."

Seb agreed that he had.

The wall behind the desk was covered with framed photos and newspaper clippings that seemed to tell the story of her career. In one photo, a younger, long-haired Angélique was accepting a trophy nearly as tall as she was. Another photo showed her shaking hands with a woman wearing a crown. And in another . . . Seb squinted. Yes, there she was with the actor who'd played James Bond. The one with the accent, just as Dragan had said.

He looked back at her and caught her watching him again. "That's pretty impressive." He pointed at the wall.

"What, that?" She glanced up as if she'd never noticed it before. "Oh, that's nothing. Just a few mementos." She beckoned for the bulldog. "This is Ennui," she said, hauling the beast up off the floor.

"*Ennui?*" Seb had to laugh. Maxime had taught him that word years ago: it was the feeling of being unimpressed and bored with life. Basically, the perfect name for the grumpy bulldog.

The directrice, however, did not laugh. In fact, she looked rather insulted. "*Henri,*" she repeated, as if he were half deaf.

"Oh. Sorry," Seb said quickly. "I heard wrong." Inwardly, he maintained that Ennui was more fitting.

The directrice cleared her throat. "Well. I'm so glad you came. And you even requested a meeting with me!

No one ever does that. What a novelty!" She laughed, and her teeth glinted, despite the low light. Seb had a vision of them glowing in the dark, like the teeth of the Cheshire Cat from *Alice in Wonderland*. He tried not to shiver.

"I was so pleased when your father finally agreed to send you," she went on. "I'd been suggesting it for ages. We're old friends, you know."

Seb nodded and tried to relax, though it was difficult on such a small, hard stool.

"How is Dragan these days?" asked Madame Saint-Germain. "It's been so long since I've seen him—fifteen years at least. I imagine he still has all his hair."

"All of it," Seb confirmed.

Angélique Saint-Germain threw back her head and laughed, and Seb joined in, though he wasn't sure why it was funny. "And the Konstantinov Family Circus is prosperous as always? I hear it's making scads of money. Mountains of it. An empire, even."

"Oh. Um . . . where did you hear that?" Seb asked, though he had a pretty good idea.

"The circus world is very small," the directrice said, stroking the skin folds on Ennui's meaty neck. The dog grumbled. "You know, I always knew your father would be a great success. It didn't surprise me when he founded his own company—he's always been a ringmaster at heart." The directrice leaned forward and looked at Seb squarely. "And what about you, Sebastian? Do you like Bonaventure? The building needs work, I know. It's an old pile of stones, constantly crumbling."

"Oh, no," Seb said quickly. "It's a beautiful place. Especially the theater."

"No." The directrice shook her head. "It's falling apart."

Seb remembered Oliver's advice. "I . . . guess it is," he said.

"Did you . . ." She lowered her voice, though there was no one around to hear her but Ennui, and he clearly couldn't care less. "Did you tell your father?"

"About what?" Seb asked.

"About the state of the school."

"Oh!" Seb started. "Of course not. I haven't talked to him at all yet. Not that I would have told him anyway. I think it's . . . a great place," he said, then he straightened on his stool. "Madame Saint-Germain, there's something I wanted to—"

"Oh." The directrice looked disappointed. "Yes, of course you haven't spoken with him yet. He's a busy man, isn't he?" She drummed her crimson fingernails on Ennui's head. The dog glowered.

"I was so heartened to hear that we were acquiring a new student with such innate talent, such skill," she said.

Seb leaned forward. "Actually, that's what I came to—"

"We have some fairly talented students at Bonaventure," she went on. "But having a Konstantinov here is a real win." She flashed him another glow-in-the-dark smile.

"Right. About that," said Seb. "What I'd like to do this year—what my dad thought would be best—is concentrate on being a circus scholar."

Angélique Saint-Germain looked puzzled. "A what?"

"A scholar," he repeated. "I want to study the modern circus. I'm sure you know that the Konstantinov Family Circus is . . ." He tried to recall her exact words in that last letter. "Too traditional. It's not keeping up with the times."

"True," she agreed. "That's what I've been telling your father for ages."

"Right," he said, encouraged. "So I have a lot of studying to do. A lot of *observing*," he added. "And I'm especially interested in the stories."

"Stories?" She cocked her head to one side, as if he'd told her he was especially interested in starting a school cricket team.

"You know, circus shows that tell stories, that aren't just about showing off skills and—"

"Yes, yes, that's one kind of show," she said, cutting him off with a wave of her hand. "Stories are fine— there's a time and a place for them. But what you of all people must understand is that circus shows would not exist were it not for exceptionally talented performers—performers who have spent tens of thousands of hours perfecting their skills. Our mission at Bonaventure is to shape the minds and bodies of young stars who will captivate audiences worldwide. And to do so, they must completely master a specific skill." She paused again to study Seb. "Tell me, Sebastian, what *is* your skill?"

"Well, I'm a kind of a circus scholar—"

"Yes, I heard you." She waved this away too. "But what is it you *do*? What is your circus *specialty*?"

"Oh." Seb squirmed. He pictured his Plan to Survive Circus School, but it was no use. A fractured metatarsal wouldn't help him now, and it was far too late to hide.

"You *do* have a specialty, don't you?" the directrice asked.

"Um," said Seb. "Well." Could he make one up? he wondered, thinking fast. Could it be something she'd never in a million years ask him to demonstrate?

Ennui looked up from Angélique Saint-Germain's lap and gave Seb a long, hard stare. It was almost more unsettling than the directrice's glow-in-the-dark teeth. Later, when pondering why on earth he'd done what he did next, Seb blamed it all on the bulldog.

"I'm . . . I'm a fire breather!" he blurted.

The directrice looked stunned—as stunned as Seb himself felt. A *fire breather*?

Then her eyes narrowed. "A fire breather," she repeated, her voice as flat as a contortionist in a guitar case.

Ennui lay his head back down with a moan.

"Fire breathing," Seb repeated, for now he'd done it and he couldn't go back. "It's all the rage in . . . Moldova."

The dog sighed, as if to tell him to stop talking, for Pete's sake.

The directrice looked like she'd just swallowed a lemon whole. "I see. Well, Sebastian, you should know that we here at Bonaventure do not breathe fire."

"Good," Seb said, relieved. "I mean, I didn't think so. I'm sure there are, like, fire safety codes or something. That's . . . why I didn't mention it before. Or bring my equipment," he added.

The directrice frowned. For a long moment, she was quiet. Then she drew a deep breath and smiled again, though not nearly as wide this time. "Well, I suppose there's not much we can do about that, is there?" She began to stroke her dog's head again. "Tell me, how is your dorm room? Who is your roommate?"

"Sylvain," he answered, relieved to change the subject.

"Sylvain . . ." She tapped Ennui's head, trying to place the name. "The juggler?"

Seb nodded.

The directrice tsked. "Unfortunate. Let me know if you get to the point of wanting to bury him alive, and I'll find you a new room. I usually get to that point with jug- glers. But they aren't nearly as bad as the contortionists." She shuddered.

"Sylvain's great," Seb assured her. "He's helped me—"

"And the room itself," she said. "Is it too small?"

"No, not at all," he said, wondering how he might wrap up this meeting. "It's perfect."

"It's very small," she told him. "And the taps leak, don't they? They're the bane of my existence. Last June a pipe exploded in the cafeteria. Water everywhere, raining down on the students, the cook, the food." She shook her head, playing with Ennui's skin folds. "A perfectly good pasta salad—ruined."

Seb was beginning to wonder if the directrice might be a little . . . unhinged. Maybe that legendary fall from the trapeze had rattled her brain?

"Will you tell your father about your room?" she asked.

"Of course not!" he exclaimed.

"Oh." She looked disappointed.

"Wait." Now Seb was very confused. "Do you *want* me to tell him?"

"No, no." She laughed. "I mean, unless, of course, you want to. I wouldn't stop you, obviously. I'm not sure what he could do, but . . ."

And suddenly, Seb understood. It struck him full force, like a fall from a swinging trapeze.

Angélique Saint-Germain had invited him to Bonaventure because the school needed money.

And as far as she knew, Dragan had money. Mountains of it. An empire, even.

Seb flushed to the roots of his hair and cringed down to his toes. He opened his mouth, then shut it, at a complete loss for words.

"Well, enough about that." She smiled again. "I should let you get back to class, and you must let me get on with my next appointment. Not nearly as enjoyable as this one, unfortunately." She leaned forward. "Bêtes noires, as we say in French. There are a few in every year, but we try to weed them out right away. There is, as I mentioned earlier, a very long wait list of deserving students, just dying to get in to Bonaventure."

"Right," Seb said weakly.

"So nice to meet you, Sebastian." The directrice rose from her throne, set Ennui on the floor, and showed Seb to the door.

11

SEB LET THE phone ring for a sixth time, knowing his father could hear it perfectly well. Dragan always kept his cell phone close by, insisting, "You never know when you might need to snap a selfie."

He also insisted that he needed his beauty sleep, which was likely what he was moaning about now, as it was past midnight wherever he was. Seb let it ring a seventh time, then an eighth. Finally, there was a click.

"Hello?" said a scratchy voice—the voice of a ringmaster, post-performance.

"Hi, Dad. Sorry to call so late."

"Seb." Dragan sighed. "What have I told you about my beauty sleep?"

"That you need it," said Seb.

"Exactly." Dragan cleared his throat. "How are you? What time is it there?"

"Dinnertime," said Seb. And though he longed for one of the bowls of spaghetti being dished out in the cafeteria down the hall, he knew this had to come first. His brain had been spinning since he'd left the directrice's office; it had taken all he had just to make it through his afternoon math and French classes.

"Dad, we need to talk," he said, sitting down on the carpet of the student lounge. It smelled like mold, but he was too tired to stand any longer. He couldn't believe it was still his first day at Bonaventure.

"All right." Seb heard his father sit down on his creaky cot, and he closed his eyes to picture it. Dragan would have washed off his show makeup and swapped his red jacket and suspenders for pajamas. Possibly he'd lacquered his hair with hot oil to maximize its shine.

"Okay," Seb said, trying to get all his thoughts organized. "First off, I want to know why everyone here thinks our circus has tons of money. And where they got the idea that it's an *empire*."

"Oh," said Dragan. "Well."

"And second," Seb continued, "I want to know who would have told them I'm charismatic. A charismatic *superstar*."

"Um," said Dragan. The cot springs squeaked. "Well, that might have been me. On both counts."

"Dad, why?" Seb wailed, but stopped when some older students sitting on the couches looked over.

"It was a long time ago!" Dragan protested. "I didn't think Angélique would ever meet you!"

"Okay." Seb took a deep breath. "Let's put the charismatic thing aside. Dad, everyone here thinks you're rolling in money."

"Do they!" Dragan sounded pleased.

"Yes. And it's not a good thing. Angélique . . ." He lowered his voice to a whisper. "Angélique Saint-Germain thinks you're going to donate money to the school."

"Donate money!" Dragan exclaimed. "Why would I do that?"

"The place needs work," said Seb. "The carpet's moldy, the paint's chipped, the stage needs patching. The lightbulbs are terrible—you'd hate them. And sometimes the pipes leak and ruin a perfectly good pasta salad. Anyway, the point is, she invited me here because she thinks you're going to support this place."

"Well. That would be very generous of me." Dragan sounded rather impressed with himself. "But I can't do it, obviously. You know that."

"Yeah." Seb wrapped the telephone cord around his wrist. "Okay, there's something else too." He drew a breath, then proceeded to tell his father about his plan to convince the directrice to let him be a circus scholar, and how it had failed royally.

"Yeesh," said Dragan.

"But it gets worse," Seb warned him. "Angélique asked me what my circus specialty was—she was positive that I had to have one. And . . . and I panicked. I told her . . ." Seb gulped. "That I breathe fire."

"Oh," said Dragan. "Oh no."

"I know, right?" Seb sighed.

"Oh, that is not good," said Dragan.

"Right but . . . but maybe it's okay," Seb said, desperate to find a bright side. "She said that students don't breathe fire at Bonaventure. There must be fire safety codes or something. So maybe I can just get away with pretending."

"Maybe," Dragan said, though he sounded doubtful. "But couldn't you have just faked an injury?"

"That was my backup plan," said Seb.

"Ah," said his father. "Did you have an injury in mind?"

"A fractured metatarsal."

"Oh, good choice."

They both fell silent, pondering the situation.

"Hey, Dad, here's a thought," Seb ventured after a few moments. "What if I just told her the truth about why I came here?"

"Nope," said Dragan. "Bad idea. The truth will only get you in trouble. They say it sets you free, but they are lying."

Seb scratched his head. "Okay, but—"

"Sebastian, you cannot tell her. You promised me. Angélique must not know about our family finances."

"Right, but I can't have her thinking—"

"Angélique can think what she wants," said Dragan. "And as for us, we might not have money, but we're going to continue on as if we do. We're going to write our own story, Sebastian. Fake it 'til we make it!"

There were roughly a hundred flaws in this plan, Seb knew. But he also knew there was no convincing his father, especially when he was missing out on his beauty sleep. "Okay," he sighed. "Tell me some news, then. How's everyone doing?"

Dragan seemed happy to change the subject. Aunt Tatiana, he reported, had dyed her beard black—or tried to, but it turned a putrid shade of olive. Meanwhile, Juan the contortionist had gotten himself stuck in a fish tank, which had made for a tense afternoon. Eventually, however, he'd dislocated all his limbs and emerged unscathed, though looking a little more angular than usual.

"Everyone's okay, then?" Seb asked, and his voice caught in his throat, thinking of them all.

"Everyone is . . . fine," said Dragan. "It's just a hard time, you know."

"I know," said Seb. "I should go, Dad."

"Okay, Seb. But please promise me one thing: that you won't ever attempt to breathe fire."

"Dad, don't worry."

"It's just that eyebrows are so important. They lend so much to a face."

"I know."

"Just try being surprised without eyebrows!"

"Okay, Dad. I got it," said Seb. And he wished his father goodnight, then hung up the phone.

BY THE TIME Seb reached his first class on the second day of school, everyone had heard the news.

"You breathe FIRE?" Camille shrieked when he emerged from the boys' change room, steeling himself once again for Basic Acrobatics with Monsieur Gerard.

"Why didn't you tell us yesterday?" Murray demanded, his voice nasal under a layer of bandages. Seb couldn't help but wish they were over his mouth.

"Most important, why didn't you tell *me?*" Sylvain asked. "We're roommates! And I had to hear it at second breakfast this morning! From a kid in third year!" He looked wounded.

"Oh. Um." Seb fumbled. "Sorry. The thing is . . . I didn't . . ."

"Perhaps Monsieur Konstantinov didn't tell us about his . . . ability," Monsieur Gerard cut in, "because fire breathing has no place at Bonaventure." All heads turned to him, including Seb's. "Breathing fire," the teacher went on, smoothing his mustache, "is part of the traditional circus, along with lion taming and bearded ladies." He curled his lip and twitched his mustache.

Seb was about to protest on behalf of all the Konstantinovs when he realized that the teacher was actually helping him. "That's true," he agreed, and all heads turned back to him. "That's why I didn't tell you. I come from a very traditional circus, and I've got a lot to learn. That's why I'm here to be a *circus scholar,*" he added for emphasis.

The students seemed to accept this—even Sylvain, though he did look a little put out.

"So how do you do it?" asked Matthieu. "How do you breathe fire?"

"Tell us everything!" cried the unicyclist duo.

"Oh. Well." Seb fumbled again, wishing he'd rehearsed this the night before; he'd been so exhausted that he'd fallen asleep as soon as his head touched the pillow. Now he tried to recall the Konstantinov fire breather—the one who'd fallen in love with an ice dancer in Saint Petersburg. "Well, you need some pretty specific gear—"

"That's enough," Monsieur Gerard snapped. "We're not here to learn about breathing fire. We're here to do acrobatics, and we're already running late." He tapped his watch. "It's time for warm-ups. Ten laps around the gym."

The students took off jogging, being careful to avoid the far west side of the gym, where an older student was having a private lesson on the tightrope. She seemed to be practicing a routine, pirouetting on the wire holding a yellow umbrella while a teacher called out directions below. Seb watched as closely as he could without tripping over the other students.

"That's Marie-Eve," Giselle said, striding beside him like a gazelle. "She's in third year."

"She's really good," Seb said as Marie-Eve took a flying leap across the line, landing with barely a wobble.

"The directrice likes her," said Giselle. "Sometimes she even lets her perform at the Friday night soirees."

Seb had forgotten about the soirees, but now he recalled the Scout suggesting that the directrice might let Seb watch one night. As much as Seb wanted to see a soiree, he didn't care to visit the directrice again. Preferably ever.

"And students are *never* allowed to perform," Camille added, catching up with them. She was skipping instead of jogging, every now and then throwing in a grand jeté, like a ballerina.

"I wonder if anyone in our year will be asked?" said Giselle.

"We will," Camille declared. "Swear on it." She held her pinkie out to Giselle, and they swore on it without breaking stride.

"Today we'll work on handstands," Monsieur Gerard announced once they'd finished their laps. "It will be second nature for some of you, and others less so. But you will all work to perfect them, no matter who you are and what your specialty is." Here he looked directly at Seb, and his mustache twitched again. "We'll work in pairs. Make sure your partner's lines are clean and their shoulders strong. Start with handstands against the wall, and if that's too easy, you can move to the mat in the center of the floor."

Seb looked to Sylvain, but his roommate had already paired up with Matthieu. Camille and Giselle were a pair, of course—not that Seb would have wanted to practice handstands with either of them.

"Partner?" someone asked, and he turned to see Frankie, who had somehow sneaked up on him without his noticing. He hesitated, but she was already walking off to the wall. Apparently, he had a partner. He hurried to catch up.

"I'll go first," Frankie when they reach the wall. And without a moment's hesitation, she lunged forward, placed her hands on the floor and kicked her legs up to meet the wall. She stood there for a few moments, looking cool and unruffled even upside down.

"So?" she said.

"Um, looks good," said Seb. She made it look so easy.

"Except you're leaning to the left," Monsieur Gerard pointed out as he passed by. "Straighten that shoulder, Frankie. This is acrobatics, not clown class."

"Harsh," Seb whispered once the teacher had moved on. But Frankie didn't seem to care. After a few more moments upside down, she let her feet drop down to the ground and popped back up.

"Your turn," she said.

"Right. So I'm really bad at this," he warned her, for there was no point in pretending. "I haven't tried handstands in years. And it didn't go well last time."

"Because you're a fire breather, not an acrobat," she said, with just a hint of a smirk.

Could Frankie see right through him? he wondered. How was that possible?

"Come on, just try it." She pointed at the wall. "I'll help."

"Okay." He tried to recall what she done, hoping maybe it was as easy as she made it seem. Or that in the few years since his last attempt, he'd somehow magically acquired the ability to stand upside down.

He licked his lips, then placed his hands on the ground and kicked up his right foot, hoping it would float up to touch the wall, followed effortlessly by his left. Just as Frankie had done.

Unsurprisingly, it did not. Instead, his foot slammed back onto the gymnasium floor. He kicked again, and again it clattered back down.

Though the blood was now rushing to his head, he tried one last time, but it was no use. He righted himself, hot with shame, and turned around slowly.

Frankie's eyes were wide. "Wow," she said. "You are really bad!" She sounded almost impressed.

"I told you," he grumbled.

"Okay, look," she said. "Here's how you learn." She got down on her hands and knees, facing away from the wall, and began to climb backwards up it. "Do this until your shoulders get a bit stronger."

Seb tried again, her way. It was a bit more doable, but it still hurt. Eventually, he collapsed on the mat, arms aching.

"Just keep working at it," she advised, flipping back up into a handstand, but without the wall to support her.

"Thanks," he said, and because she looked rather peaceful like that, and not nearly as intimidating as usual, he asked, "So how did it go yesterday with the directrice?"

"Well, I'm still alive, so that's a win." Frankie stood on one hand, then the other. "I got a warning, so I'm on probation. Two more warnings and I lose my place to one of the many deserving wait-listed students who are just dying to get into Bonaventure." Even upside down, Frankie's imitation of the directrice was spot on. Seb laughed, then looked around to make sure Monsieur Gerard wasn't listening.

But the teacher was busy reprimanding Banjo Brady, who had just slipped in, late again.

"He got a warning too," Frankie said, flipping over onto her feet. "He's not allowed outside ever. And he has to start getting to class on time. *Or else.*"

They watched Banjo hurry off to the change room. Then Frankie said, "We're going to be the only ones here on the weekends, you know."

"Huh?" Seb turned back to her.

"You're going to stay here on weekends, right?"

He nodded.

"I heard that most kids don't," said Frankie. "They go home if they live close by, or they stay with host families. But you, Banjo and I will be staying here. The bêtes noires," she added.

"I'm not a—" he began. But he stopped, for Frankie was smirking again, and he had no desire to argue with her. Instead, he turned to watch Marie-Eve, the third-year tightrope walker, who had just sunk into the splits on top of the line. High above her, he noticed, there was a large window, and in it stood the directrice, holding the meaty Ennui in her arms and watching the scene below.

Except she wasn't watching the tightrope walker or any of the students standing on their hands.

She was staring right at Seb and Frankie. And she did not look pleased.

12

THAT FIRST WEEK at Bonaventure felt like three. By the time Friday afternoon arrived, Seb was completely exhausted; it was all he could do to drag himself to the student lounge and sprawl on a couch while the other students streamed out the front door to the cars awaiting them. He felt a small stab of envy thinking about the hot dinners they'd enjoy at home, while he had a few days of cold cafeteria food ahead of him. But mostly he just wanted to be left alone, to sleep and read and think about his predicament.

"Hey, Superstar." Sylvain plunked down beside him. The old couch springs squeaked. "Want this?" He held up his bag of candy—or what was left of it.

"Really?" Seb said. "You don't want it?"

"My mom has loads more at home," Sylvain assured him. "I'll just bring more on Monday."

Seb felt another small stab. He wondered if Sylvain's mother was anything like Aunt Tatiana—minus the obvious facial hair.

"Well, have a good weekend!" Sylvain jumped back up. "Oh, and watch out for the directrice. I hear she stays around some weekends." He turned and jogged out the door.

Seb sighed. "Great."

Soon the front door slammed shut one final time, and Bonaventure fell quiet—deeply quiet. Seb could even hear the drip of a leaky pipe in the cafeteria.

Frankie had been right: barely any students stayed around on weekends. And there was only one teacher supervisor, but who knew where they were? It would be easy, Seb decided, to go the entire weekend without running into anyone.

Which sounded just about perfect.

He headed first to the cafeteria to get a sandwich for dinner. But as he passed the gymnasium, he noticed a light on inside. He paused to peek in and spotted Banjo Brady, dressed in his usual grass-stained jeans and a plaid shirt.

As Seb watched, Banjo secured a flat nylon rope between two posts. Then he kicked off his sneakers, wiggled his toes and hopped up onto the line.

Arms spread wide, Banjo took a few tentative steps on his slackline, then bent his knees so he could bounce when the line bounced and sway when it swayed. A soft, half-smile appeared on his face, and suddenly, he looked totally, completely at peace.

"It's called the state of 'flow,'" Seb remembered Maxime once explaining. "It happens when a person is completely immersed in what they're doing, whether that's juggling pins or swinging on a trapeze. It could even be baking a cake or writing a song."

"Or swallowing sharp medieval weapons?" Seb had asked.

"Even that," Max confirmed. "It's hard to describe, but I swear to you, it's the very best feeling in the world."

"I've never felt it before." Of this, Seb was certain.

"You will," Maxime promised.

Now Seb's chest felt tight again, so he stepped away from the door, no longer just wanting but *needing* to be by himself. He dashed to the cafeteria, grabbed a sandwich and was heading up to his room when suddenly, he remembered the choir box.

He did an about-face and headed for the theater. Thankfully, its doors were unlocked, practically inviting him to come inside.

It was just as wonderful as he remembered it: grand and stately and tranquil all at once. Rainbow light from the stained glass windows played upon the scratched

floors. The saints stood at attention under marble arch-
ways.

What a space for circus shows! Seb marveled once
again. If he were in charge, he'd put on a production about
ghosts, starring aerial silks performers dressed in white.
He pictured them tumbling from the ceiling, stopping
their fall just inches above the audience's heads.

For the first time all week, he felt content.

He headed for the staircase at the back of the theater.
A rope still cordoned off the stairs, but he stepped over it
and climbed up. At the top of the stairs, he let himself into
the choir box and looked around. It was a small space—
big enough for only three or four musical monks. But it
was just perfect for Seb.

He stretched out on his back, watching the dust dance
in the rafters. "Finally," he sighed. Time to think.

He started by taking stock of the week. On the one
hand, he hadn't been sent home, forced to give up his
place to one of the more deserving students on the wait
list. So that, as Frankie said, was a win.

On the other hand, he *had* gone and convinced everyone at Bonaventure that he could breathe fire. This was
not exactly a foolproof situation, especially because
everyone now wanted details. He'd have to do some
research so he could answer them convincingly.

He sighed. Lying was exhausting. He had no idea how his father kept it up.

He was trying to remember details from the Konstantinov fire breather's routine when he heard the theater door creak open. He sat upright, hoping he'd heard wrong. But a moment later, he heard it close, and soft footsteps tiptoe in.

"Oh no," he whispered, praying whoever it was would leave. But the footsteps tiptoed on in . . . and over to the staircase.

And then they were climbing the stairs.

Seb scuttled backwards, heart pounding. He tucked himself into a corner, though of course it wouldn't hide him. He was very much trapped.

Then the door to the choir box opened, and a figure appeared, backlit by the rainbow light. A tall, skinny figure topped with a rat's nest of hair.

Frankie de Luca.

"You!" she exclaimed.

"You!" he returned.

"What are you doing here?" she demanded.

"I could ask you the same thing," he pointed out, sliding out of the corner as casually as possible, as if he'd just been curled up there for a nap.

"This is my hiding spot," Frankie said. "It's perfect, see?

No one can bother me up here." Then she frowned at him, as if to say, "until now."

This annoyed him—she couldn't just claim it as her own. "It's my hiding spot too," he informed her.

She stared at him for a moment, then shrugged and sat down. "So you're here to watch the show?"

"What show?" he asked.

"The soiree," she said.

"Oh!" He hadn't even thought about it. "But we aren't allowed to watch the shows, are we?" he said.

"We're not invited," she corrected him. "That doesn't mean we can't watch."

He wasn't sure about the logic, but once again he decided not to argue with her.

"I guess we'll watch it together then." She leaned against a wall and stretched out her legs, which were so long they took up nearly half the box.

This was definitely not the Friday evening Seb had had in mind. He considered taking his candy and heading for the library, or back to his room. But then the theater door swung open again, and in tromped a half-dozen riggers, chatting in French. Minutes later, they were testing the lights and setting up a trapeze.

Seb sighed. They were trapped. And what's more, now he'd have to share his candy—he couldn't very well keep it all to himself. Grudgingly, he pulled out Sylvain's bag and pushed it toward Frankie.

Her eyes lit up. "Where did you get that?"

"Can't reveal my sources," he told her, taking the last gummy bear for himself.

"Mysterious," she said, grabbing a string of licorice. She sounded like she approved.

They chewed in silence for a moment, then Frankie said, "So this fire breathing thing. Is that real?"

He coughed and swallowed. He hadn't expected this. "Of course."

"Be honest," she warned him. "I've got three little brothers—I can smell a lie from a mile away."

"I'm not lying," he snapped, then remembered the riggers below and lowered his voice. "I'm . . . I'm a fire breather. Or, I used to be. I'm . . . retired now."

He was beginning to wonder whether he'd actually inherited his father's talent for making up stories.

She grinned and shook her head, clearly unconvinced. "All right, Fire Breath. Whatever you say. But you *definitely* got in without an audition."

There was no point in denying that one: she'd seen his handstands. "Nice work, Detective," he said.

She laughed. "They didn't make me audition either."

"Really?" Seb recalled the Scout's brief story of how he'd discovered her. "So the Scout just found you? Doing parkour in Rome?" It sounded just as odd as the Scout discovering Banjo at Stumpville's Logger Sports Day.

"Pretty much." Frankie leaned forward and touched her toes. "I wish I could be outside doing parkour right now. I would be if I weren't on probation." She looked up at the ceiling rafters as if considering scaling them. "Parkour is the best way to explore a new place."

Personally, Seb preferred a map. But he let it go, and helped himself to more candy.

At seven thirty, the theater went dark, then some soft stage lights came up, along with beams of red and purple in the rafters. The riggers finished hanging some silks and disappeared behind the curtain. Then the music began—wavering wind instruments and faint, thumping percussion. It was nothing like the tinny orchestral march that opened the Konstantinov Family Circus, but Seb still felt the familiar pre-show thrill, anticipating the magic to come.

His watch read ten to eight when the theater doors opened again, and in came the circophiles of Montreal.

Peering over the side of the box, Seb did a double take. "What the?"

"Whoa," Frankie breathed, crouched beside him. "What are they *wearing*?"

The answer seemed to be "pretty well anything." Some wore fancy suits, others shimmering gowns and high heels. Still others looked as if they were headed to a costume party; Seb spotted one woman dressed head to toe in shiny green snakeskin, another wearing a birdcage on her head, and a man who'd waxed his mustache to stand out like cat whiskers, which complemented the furry ears atop his head.

"Who are these people?" Frankie wondered. Seb had no idea.

The music swelled, and a swarm of servers emerged from behind the statues, carrying trays of skinny glasses filled with some violet-colored concoction. They wove between the circophiles, who helped themselves. Soon everyone was laughing and drinking as they complimented each other's outfits.

The show began with a trapeze act—a lone woman tipping and twirling above the audience's heads. She was skilled and strong, Seb noted as he watched her hang from the trapeze by just her neck—the same trick that Maria the Konstantinov aerialist was working on. But her routine was just that: a series of tricks, and no story.

What's more, the circophiles weren't even watching. They strutted around, preening like exotic birds, more interested in each other than the performance above their heads.

"Don't trapezes usually swing?" Frankie asked. "I

thought trapezists were supposed to fly across the room and catch each other."

"This is the static trapeze," Seb explained. "It doesn't move much, so it's all up to the artist to make shapes that look impressive." They watched as the woman flipped back up to sit on the bar. "It takes a ton of strength, but a good performer will make it look easy."

"Have you tried it?" Frankie asked.

Seb nodded, recalling how Maria had had to heave him up onto the bar, since he wasn't strong enough to pull himself up. Once he was up there, it became very clear to him how very high he was, and how many bones he might break if he fell.

"Um, I think I'm done," he'd said. Maria took one look at his terrified eyes and agreed. The trapeze was not for him.

"Think Murray's really a trapeze master?" asked Frankie.

"I doubt it," said Seb. "Mastering the trapeze takes more hours than he's been alive."

They fell silent again, watching the show. After the trapezist came a tightrope act, then some silks performers. All were skilled, but no more so than Maria. And none of the acts seemed to tell a story, which for Seb was more than a little disappointing.

Still, he concluded, there were worse ways to spend a Friday night than polishing off a bag of candy while watching a circus show from a secret hiding spot.

A hiding spot, he had to admit, that actually was big enough for two.

Part 3

BÊTES NOIRES

13

OR A TIME, it seemed like Seb's fire breathing excuse was going to work. He used it tentatively at first, murmuring it to the juggling teacher when asked to demonstrate a three-ball cascade, and later to the aerials instructor, who assumed he'd be a natural on the silks.

"You're a what?" The juggling teacher looked alarmed.

"*Mon Dieu!*" The aerials instructor grimaced outright.

"Yes." Seb nodded ruefully. "My circus is pretty outdated. That's why I'm here: to learn the ways of the modern circus."

The juggling teacher shook his head in wonder. The aerials instructor shuddered.

"Take a seat, then," both told him.

It was almost too easy.

He did, however, sneak off to the library one night to brush up on his fire breathing knowledge, just in case. And he found it was as he remembered. The gist of breathing fire was pretty simple: it required a fuel source, a flame and a disconcerting lack of fear.

Basically, the performer would take a swig of fuel, hold it in his mouth, then spray it over an open flame, which would make the flame burst into some striking shape, like a giant pillar or a ball of fire. So he wasn't truly breathing fire, but just creating the illusion of it.

Unsurprisingly, there were untold ways the performer could muck things up. He might spray his fuel in the wrong direction, or with the wrong consistency (a fine mist was best). The flame might balloon out of control or blow back toward him. And, of course, he could accidentally swallow the fuel, which would make him very sick, if not kill him outright.

When you broke it down, Seb concluded, fire breathing was full-on bonkers.

But it made an effective excuse, and so he kept on using it. Sometimes he'd even embellish it a little with stories he remembered the Konstantinov fire breather telling—like how he'd once misjudged the direction of the wind and received a faceful of flames.

By the end of Seb's first month at Bonaventure, telling this story had begun to feel almost normal.

The daily routine was feeling normal as well. From Monday through Friday, the fifteen first-year students were nearly always together. They ate breakfast elbow to elbow each morning, raced each other to the cafeteria at lunchtime and haggled over the couches in the student lounge, where many did their homework every evening.

And then on Friday afternoon, as soon as the last bell rang, they were gone, streaming out to the waiting cars, letting the front doors slam shut behind them. Sylvain would always leave Seb what remained of his weekly candy bag, which Seb would take up to the choir box to watch the Friday soiree, both for the acts and to see what the circophiles were wearing. Sometimes Frankie came too, if she wasn't busy practicing her parkour moves in the gymnasium.

Seb, however, never set foot in the gym on weekends. For one thing, there was really no point in practicing his skills. But more important, he didn't want Angélique Saint-Germain to see him. It seemed that whenever he looked up during Juggling or Aerials or Basic Acrobatics, there she'd be, surveying the scene from her window with Ennui in her arms.

And perhaps it was just his imagination, but she always seemed to be watching *him*, even when there were fourteen other students around. It made him cringe, which in turn made him mess up whichever skill he was attempting. He had no idea what she was thinking while she watched him, and he didn't particularly want to find out.

But of course, it was only a matter of time before he did.

It was a Friday morning in late September, crisp and clear—or so it seemed through the little window in Room Number 5. Seb had yet to actually venture outside, which was getting a little tiresome. He'd tried on a few occasions to coerce the weekend supervisor into taking him out exploring, but someone always had to stay with Banjo Brady, who wasn't ever allowed outside. So as a result, Seb still knew next to nothing about Montreal.

On that Friday morning, he arrived at Basic Acrobatics and found an odd sight: the Scout and Monsieur Gerard arguing. Or rather, Monsieur Gerard was arguing; the Scout was listening to him patiently, nodding every now and then or humming with sympathy. Seb wondered if the Scout had dabbled as a therapist as well.

"Basic Acrobatics," Monsieur Gerard was proclaiming, "is the most important class these students attend. I have too much to teach them to give up an entire class for the sake of one student!"

"I know." The Scout gave him a gentle smile. "But it's not for one student. You know that. It's for *her*."

Monsieur Gerard opened his mouth to argue, then snapped it shut.

"For who?" asked Camille.

"Who do you think?" said Sylvain.

Before she could guess, the door swung open, and in walked one of the riggers, carrying a crate full of some sort of equipment.

It was an odd assembly of objects, Seb noted: a few bottles, some long sticks, gloves, a tarp, and—

He froze. A few bottles . . . some long sticks . . .

"No. Way," he breathed.

"No way what?" Sylvain turned to him.

But Seb couldn't answer, for he felt like he'd been socked in the gut. If he was correct, and he was fairly certain he was, those long sticks were torches. And those bottles held fuel.

She was going to make him breathe fire.

The door swung open again, and Seb whirled around to face her. But it was only Banjo Brady, late, as usual. He stammered an apology, but no one seemed to hear it—least of all Seb, who couldn't hear anything over the hammering of his heart.

He'd just resolved to make a break for it, to sprint back up to his dorm and fake a sudden flu, when the door opened a third time, and in swept the directrice herself.

Ennui trudged along behind her, looking like he was being kept from his breakfast.

The class gasped.

"What's she doing here?" Giselle whispered.

"I'm wearing my worst leotard!" Camille moaned.

"Angélique." Monsieur Gerard stepped forward, smoothing his mustache. "What an honor." He air-kissed her on each cheek.

"I know it is," she agreed. "I so rarely grace a class with my presence. Especially not a first-year class," she added, flashing the students a blinding smile. "But today is a special occasion—a surprise for one of our students!"

Please no, Seb begged her silently.

But she turned her smile directly on him, like the beam of a searchlight. "I thought about warning you, Sebastian. But then I remembered that you're a Konstantinov. And a Konstantinov is always ready to perform!"

Nooooo! he screamed silently.

"He's going to perform?" asked Sylvain. "But he's—"

"A fire breather!" Angélique Saint-Germain finished. "Exactly. And he's going to show us all his skills."

The students gasped again.

"You are?" said Camille.

"Cool!" Sylvain shouted.

"Here?" asked one of the unicyclists. "Aren't there fire codes?"

"Don't worry," the Scout assured her. "I've dabbled in firefighting."

The students murmured excitedly—all except Frankie, who was staring at Seb, eyes wide and full of concern.

"All right then." Monsieur Gerard shook his head, resigned. "Sit down, everyone. Hopefully this won't take long, and we can get back to perfecting our cartwheels."

"We've gathered everything you need, Sebastian." Angélique Saint-Germain gestured to the crate. "So I suppose I'll just turn it over to you. Show us what it is you do best." She gave him a long look, and Seb understood that this was a test—that after four weeks of watching him, she rightfully didn't believe he had any circus skills at all.

"Um." He looked at the students now seated in front of him, then at the teachers standing close behind. "Well." He had no idea what to do.

Slowly, he walked over to the crate and peered inside. Just as he'd feared, it was all there, everything he needed to breathe fire, except the disconcerting lack of fear.

"Well," he said again. "Um."

He closed his eyes and pictured the Konstantinov fire breather in action, swishing his mouth with lighter fluid, spitting it out between his teeth and onto a torch, turning a tiny flame into a great plume of fire.

For a moment, he wondered, Can I actually do this?

Eyebrows, Sebastian, warned his father's voice in his head. *They lend so much to a face.*

He looked back at his audience. The students were waiting patiently. Monsieur Gerard was smoothing his mustache over and over. Angélique Saint-Germain was watching Seb in a way that reminded him of the Konstantinov lion before dinnertime. Ennui lay at her feet, incapable of caring any less.

He noticed Frankie slip off to the girls' change room, likely not wanting to witness the impending disaster. He couldn't blame her.

He turned back to the crate, picked up a torch, then uncapped one of the bottles. The smell made him gag. Who in their right mind would put fuel *in their mouth?*

Could *he?*

Could he?

He dropped the torch back into the crate. There was no way. He was beaten.

"What's wrong, Sebastian?" the directrice asked.

"I can't do it," he said quietly.

"And why is that?" Angélique Saint-Germain asked, a note of triumph in her voice.

Seb turned to face his classmates, his teachers, the directrice and her nasty little bulldog. "I'm not a fire breather," he told them.

The class gasped again.

"Wait, what?" said Murray.

"So what you're telling us is that you lied," the directrice snapped.

"Now, Angélique." The Scout stepped forward.

"Don't Angélique me," she told him. "I told you this would happen. Didn't I say all along that—"

But they didn't get to find out what she'd said all along. For at that moment, a new sound sliced through the air, drowning out all the students' murmurs and the directrice's shouts.

It was the sound of the Bonaventure fire alarm.

14

B Y TEN O'CLOCK that morning, the bêtes noires were lined up, once again, on the bench outside the directrice's office. This time, Banjo was in for being late to class fourteen times in the first month of school, Seb for pretending to be a fire breather to avoid practicing circus skills, and Frankie for pulling the fire alarm in an attempt to save Seb from setting his face on fire.

"I still can't believe you did that," Seb murmured as they waited for the directrice to call them into her office.

"You were about to put lighter fluid in your mouth," said Frankie. "Even my littlest brother, Pio, knows not to do that. And you should *see* some of the stuff he puts in his mouth."

"You might have died," Banjo agreed.

Over at his too-small desk, Bruno paused in his typing. "You still might," he pointed out, with a nod toward the directrice's door. "You all might, actually." Then he resumed his typing.

"Thanks," Seb told him. "That's helpful."

He turned back to Frankie. "Anyway, you should blame me," he told her. "If the directrice wants to send you back to Rome for pulling the fire alarm, blame me."

Frankie leaned back against the wall and closed her eyes. "I intend to."

The phone on Bruno's desk rang, and he snatched it up. "*Oui, Madame,*" he said, then hung up. "Sebastian Konstantinov," he announced. "Once again, you are first in line." He sounded rather amused.

The directrice, however, was not.

"I am not amused, Sebastian," she told him as he slunk across her office, past the grand piano and the bust of her head. Ennui lay on a velvet cushion beside her desk, snoring like an elephant with a sinus infection.

"I'm sorry," Seb began, perching on the stool across from her throne.

"I am not amused," she repeated, louder this time. "But neither am I surprised. Clearly, lying runs in the family. This fiasco has Konstantinov written all over it."

"Oh, no, I—" Seb began to protest.

"You are your father's son," Madame Saint-Germain went on. "Except for one thing. You, Sebastian, are not a circus performer."

Somehow, no matter how often he'd heard it, it never hurt any less. He looked down at his sneakers. "I know."

"So I suppose you take after your mother."

His head snapped back up. "My mother? You *know* her?"

"Not really," she replied. "I never met her. In fact, I never even received a wedding invitation, despite all those years your father and I trained together." She sniffed. "Well, I knew it wouldn't last. She wasn't a circus person. I don't know why Dragan thought that was a good match."

"Wait, so what happened?" Seb asked, momentarily forgetting the fire-breathing fiasco. "Do you know where she is?"

"Don't you?" Angélique Saint-Germain raised an eyebrow.

He shook his head.

"Well, I can't remember." She stood up from her throne and went over to Ennui's cushion. The dog growled when she picked him up, but she hauled him back to the throne to sit in her lap. "I believe she just went back to her old life, to become a pharmacist or an insurance agent—something pedestrian." The directrice shrugged. "But back to the point, Sebastian. The point is, you lied to me."

"Right but—" Seb wasn't finished asking about his mother.

"You lied to everyone," she went on. "And I won't have that. We here at the Bonaventure Circus School are like a family. We share in the school's successes and wallow together in its failures. And families are bonded by trust. Tell me, Sebastian." She leaned forward over Ennui. "Do you want to be part of this family?"

"Yes!" he cried, though not because he really wanted another family. Bonaventure was still his only chance to save the Konstantinovs. "I really do."

She sighed, and Ennui echoed it. "You are putting me in a very hard place here, Sebastian. What you did was dishonest. Deceitful. *Fraudulent*, even. I have every reason to send you home to . . ." She waved her hand vaguely. "Wherever the Konstantinovs are these days."

"Slovakia, I think," said Seb.

She grimaced. "But I will not do that."

"You won't?"

"No. Or rather, not yet. I will, however, put you on probation. And that means your continued presence at Bonaventure depends on three things." She held up her hand to count on her crimson fingernails. "One: you must practice your skills. Every day. Even the ones you are terrible at. *Especially* those."

Seb gulped. "Okay."

"Two: you must excel in your academic classes. And by that I mean straight As."

He nodded. "Got it."

"And three: you must contribute to the Bonaventure Circus School."

"Contribute," he repeated, unsure what she meant.

"Contribute."

"Like . . . tidying up the common room?"

"That is not what I mean," she told him.

"I see," he said.

"Do you?"

"No."

She looked like she wanted to stuff him into a guitar case. "Sebastian," she said. "As you can see, Bonaventure is in a bad way. And it will get worse if we do not find a champion. A patron. A *philanthropist*, even."

"Oh." Seb realized what she meant.

"Do you understand what I'm saying?" she asked.

"Yes," he said. "But here's the thing—"

"Good," said Angélique Saint-Germain. "Then I will leave you to decide how to proceed." She waved toward the door. "You may go now."

Seb didn't move. More than anything, he wanted to tell her the truth: that the Konstantinovs were deeply in the crimson, and Dragan was the furthest thing from a philanthropist.

The truth will not set you free, his father's voice warned. *They say it will, but they are lying.*

But telling lies is worse! he argued silently. Didn't you see what happened this morning? I almost put lighter fluid *in my mouth!*

"Look," he said to the directrice. "There's something you should know."

She raised an eyebrow. Ennui lifted his head and gave Seb a look that seemed to say, "You're really going to do this?"

Was he? Seb paused to envision the outcome of telling the truth. She'd probably have him on a plane to Slovakia by the end of the day, probably on his father's dime. And his father didn't even *have* a dime.

And that would effectively ruin his chances of saving the Konstantinov Family Circus. He'd be right back where he started.

"Sebastian," said the directrice, "I do not have all day. What is it that I need to know?"

"Um, that I'll try," he said. "To do what you said."

"Good," she said. "Now please send in the next one on your way out."

"Okay." He stood up, then paused. "Sorry, which one?"

She rolled her eyes. "Good point. Let's have the de Luca delinquent. Honestly, the fire alarm? What was she think—" Suddenly her eyes widened. "Oh!" she said. "She did it . . . for you!"

"Um," Seb said, unsure whether agreeing would get Frankie in more trouble. "Maybe . . . ?"

"She did." The directrice nodded. "Sebastian, a word of advice: stay away from those bêtes noires. You're better than them. If only a little."

He wasn't sure what to say to that.

"Send me Frankie de Luca," she commanded, and he did as he was told.

15

WHEN SEB REJOINED his classmates, he kept his head low and tried to ignore their stares. Not in the mood for conversation, he spent lunchtime in the library, reading *Escape from the Haunted Prison*. It was, as Oliver had promised, a great story. But it did nothing to improve his mood.

Fortunately, his afternoon classes were math, science and English, none of which required him to talk. He noted that Frankie and Banjo were similarly quiet when they returned to class as well. But at least they too had survived their second trip to the directrice's office without getting shipped home. For now, anyway.

After school, when the students began streaming for the front door and the waiting cars, Seb headed straight to his room. But when he opened the door to Room Number 5, he came face-to-face with Sylvain.

"Oh. Um. Hi," Seb said.

"Hey, Super—" Sylvain began, then stopped himself. For of course, he couldn't say *that* anymore.

Seb blushed. Sylvain shrugged and began stuffing dirty laundry into a bag to bring home.

Seb darted over to his bed, grabbed his copy of *Escape from the Haunted Prison*, then turned to hurry back out again. But when he reached the door, he stopped; it didn't seem right to not talk to Sylvain. He was, after all, one of the nicest people Seb had met. "Hey, I'm sorry," he said. "For lying."

Sylvain took a whiff of a sock, gagged a bit, then shoved it in his bag. "It's okay," he said.

"Is it?" asked Seb.

"Well, it's kind of weird," Sylvain admitted, looking up from his laundry. "So you're not a performer at all?"

"Nope," Seb said. "I have no skills."

"Nothing?"

"Nada."

"Huh." Sylvain contemplated this as he knotted the top of his laundry bag. "So you were unmasked."

"Sorry?"

"Like in clown class," Sylvain explained. "Audrey's always talking about how people need to take off the masks they wear every day in order to find their inner clowns. You, my friend, were unmasked."

"I guess so," Seb said. It sounded about right, though it certainly hadn't brought him any closer to finding his inner clown.

"Yes." Sylvain nodded wisely. Then he paused again. "So . . . why are you here then? I mean, no offense, but how did you get into Bonaventure without any skills?"

Seb blushed.

"Oh," said Sylvain. "Your dad, right?"

Seb couldn't deny it.

"Right." Sylvain frowned at his laundry bag, and Seb could tell he thought this unfair. Sylvain had friends on the Bonaventure wait list, after all—friends deserving of the place Seb had been granted. He picked up his book, ready to leave again.

"Do you even want to be here?" Sylvain asked.

"Of course!" said Seb. "I was the one who decided to come, without my dad even knowing. I really want to be here. And I want to stay."

Sylvain considered this for a moment, and Seb could tell he didn't really understand. But Seb couldn't explain any more without giving away the Konstantinov family secrets. He stayed quiet.

"Well, I guess that's good," Sylvain said eventually. He lifted his bag of laundry up and placed it atop his head. "Now, most important, what was it like?"

"What was what like?"

"Going to her office. Was it as scary as they say?"

Seb considered this. "I'd say it was worse."

Sylvain gave a low whistle. "Glad you survived. Here." With his laundry balanced on top of his head, he opened his drawer, pulled out his bag of candy and tossed it to Seb. "I left you some jawbreakers this time. They're my favorite."

Seb had never felt so grateful. "Thank you," he told his roommate.

"Have a good weekend," Sylvain said, and he teetered out of the room, leaving Seb with a half-eaten bag of candy that felt like a great gift.

As soon as the last student had left, he took the candy and his book and headed for the choir box. Inside the theater, he tiptoed up the stairs and settled in, wondering if Frankie would join him. On the one hand, he wanted very badly to know what had happened to her in the directrice's office. On the other hand, though, it was a relief to be alone.

He tried to read *Escape from the Haunted Prison*, but his mind kept wandering, so he put it aside, closed his eyes and did what he now did whenever he was having a particularly bad day, or simply needed an escape. He returned to the story of the animals escaping the Bucharest Zoo.

But he hadn't even gotten past the part where the monkey picked the locks to spring the animals free when he heard the theater door open and someone tiptoe in.

Frankie. He sat up and moved over, making room for her ridiculously long legs.

"This way."

Seb sat upright. It was Frankie all right, but who was with her?

"Watch that sixth step. It's pretty rotten."

Before Seb could ask what the heck she was doing, Frankie appeared at the top of the stairs, with Banjo Brady beside her.

"Oh," said Seb.

"I brought Banjo," Frankie announced, though this was quite clear.

"Hi," Banjo said nervously. "Am I allowed up here?"

Seb sighed. Though he didn't particularly want to share his hiding space with yet another person, he couldn't very well say no to Banjo. "Sure," he said, moving over to make room for three.

"Thanks," said Banjo, tucking himself into a corner. "I heard that Marie-Eve from third year is performing tonight, and I'd love to see her tightrope routine. The Scout thinks I should take up the tightrope. Well, if I get to stay," he added.

"So what happened today?" Seb asked.

Frankie held up a hand. "Candy first. Then we debrief."

"Bossy," Seb muttered, but he pulled out the candy bag anyway.

"I got my second warning," Banjo explained once they each had a jawbreaker the size of a juggling ball. "She said she'll give me one month to stop being late to class. If I can't do it, she'll ship me back to Stumpville."

"You still haven't found your . . . what did you call it?" Frankie asked.

"Internal compass." Banjo shook his head mournfully. "I'm scared it's gone forever."

"I bet it isn't," Seb said, though he still didn't really know what an internal compass was, much less how to find one that had gone missing. He turned to Frankie. "What happened to you?"

"I got a second warning too," she said. "One more for bad behavior, and I'm back to Rome. Oh, and I have to start doing better in French class." She shrugged and slurped her jawbreaker, as if she didn't care.

Before Seb could ask what the directrice had said about the fire alarm fiasco, Frankie turned to him. "So what about *you*?"

"Well, I'm on probation," he admitted. "I might get sent home too."

"You?" Banjo gaped. "But you're the superstar!"

"Except I'm not," said Seb. "At all. I'm not a fire breather or anything else. I have zero circus skills."

Frankie nodded, as if she'd known it all along. Banjo, however, looked shocked. "But you grew up in a circus!"

"Yeah," said Seb. "But that doesn't mean I'm meant to perform." He recalled what the directrice had said about his mother. Maybe if he failed out of Bonaventure, he would try for dental school or pharmacy. Something pedestrian. "Anyway, I've got to practice all my skills and excel in my academic classes, or else I'm out." He omitted the part about getting his father to support the school—he didn't even want to think about that.

They all fell silent, sucking their jawbreakers.

"The way I see it," Frankie said after a moment, "we only have one option."

"For what?" asked Seb.

"Survival," she said. "We need to work together as a team."

"We do?" Banjo looked hopeful.

Frankie nodded. "We're all bêtes noires, after all." And she looked at Seb, as if daring him to deny that he was one of them.

He couldn't. Not anymore.

"But how?" asked Banjo.

"I don't know yet," Frankie said, swapping her jawbreaker for a chocolate caramel. "But I know that there's strength in numbers. We'll come up with a plan."

The theater door swung open again, and in tromped the stagehands and riggers, to prepare for the soiree. Seb sat back against the wall, thinking about his original Plan to Survive Circus School and what this next one might look like, with all of them drawing it up together. It reminded him of his homemade map of Eastern Europe, and all those hours he and Maxime had spent sketching it. If only he could make a map that showed the path to circus school survival, he mused.

Which gave him an interesting idea.

16

AFTER BREAKFAST ON Saturday morning, the bêtes noires met in the library to make Banjo a homemade map of the Bonaventure Circus School.

"Okay." Seb spread out some paper and pencils on a table. "Let's start by sketching each floor. Then we'll add in the details. And these can be anything," he added, because that's what Maxime had told him, all those years ago. "Anything you find weird or interesting about the school. Draw it in."

"Okay!" Banjo grabbed a pencil and got started.

Frankie, however, insisted on tackling her French homework first, so she scribbled in her notebook while the boys sketched.

"Is this where the clown classroom goes?" Banjo asked.

"It's around the corner," Seb told him.

"Really?" Banjo sketched it in.

"That's too small," Frankie observed. "Audrey's classroom is at least twice as big. And don't forget her office next door."

Seb raised an eyebrow at her, then looked pointedly at a pencil.

"Not now," she said. "Banjo, that's not where the stairwell goes. It's over—"

Seb picked up a pencil and held it out. She eyed it for a moment, then snatched it up.

"Let me show you," she said, nudging them out of the way.

They drew all the hallways and classrooms, offices and dorm rooms. They drew bathrooms and stairwells and storage closets. Then they added in odd things they'd noticed, like the water fountain that spurted right in your face. And the table in the cafeteria with the crooked leg that would occasionally collapse, leaving some kid with egg salad in their lap.

"Don't forget the choir box," said Frankie. Seb added that to the theater.

"And the rotten sixth step," added Banjo.

Seb drew the stair, with an arrow and a note of caution.

"And the statue in the theater that looks like Monsieur Gerard," said Frankie.

"What?" The boys looked at her. "That doesn't exist."

"It does," Frankie insisted. "It's right in this corner." She grabbed Seb's pencil and quickly sketched a statue with a dour, pinched look on its mustachioed face—a surprisingly accurate representation of the acrobatics teacher. Banjo and Seb burst into laughter.

"You've got skills," Seb commended her.

"I've had some practice," Frankie said.

"Did you take art classes?" asked Banjo.

Frankie shook her head. "Self-taught," she said.

"Like with parkour," said Banjo.

Frankie shrugged. "Kind of." Then she went on to sketch the other saints' faces, each as detailed as the first.

Hours passed, and they barely noticed them. By lunchtime, they had made an enormous map of the Bonaventure Circus School.

"That should do it," Frankie said, surveying their work. "Right, Banjo?"

"I hope so," he said, rolling up the map. "I'll study it a bit every day."

Seb watched him take the map up to his room, feeling rather pleased with himself. He'd just decided to celebrate by finishing *Escape from the Haunted Prison* when Frankie let out a big sigh.

"What's up?" he asked.

"French." She grimaced at her notebook. "I'm supposed to be writing a paragraph describing my family."

Seb sat back down. "Do you know any French?"

"Of course," she sniffed. "Do *you*?"

He nodded. "Let's see." He took her notebook and read over the few sentences she'd written. He was fairly certain she was describing her three little brothers, but it was hard to tell—partly because her grammar was awful, and partly because the three sentences she'd written contained a half-dozen colorful swearwords and insults.

"Frankie!" he cried. "You can't write this!"

"Why not?" she asked.

"Because it's really rude!"

"Really?" Frankie peered at the paper.

"Yes! Look, this is a bad one." He pointed at a word he recalled Maxime using once when he dropped the hilt of a broadsword on his foot. "And whoa, where'd you learn this one?"

"From the tourists in Rome," she replied. "That's where I learned all my French."

He shook his head. "Those must have been some angry tourists."

"You have no idea," said Frankie. "Anyway, can you help me fix it?"

Seb thought longingly about the haunted prison. But if, as Frankie said, their only chance at survival was to become a team . . .

He picked up a pencil again. "Okay, let's do it."

The day zipped by. By the end of it, Banjo had a home-made map, Frankie had pages of French homework completed, *sans* swear words, and Seb still hadn't read his book. But he was oddly okay with that. There was always Sunday.

On Sunday, however, they intercepted him right after breakfast, on his way to the library.

"You're coming with us," Frankie told him, and she and Banjo each took hold of one of his arms.

"I am?" he said, thoroughly confused. "Where?"

"The gym," said Frankie. "Now it's time to work on *your* homework."

"Oh, no!" Seb dug in his heels. "Guys, there's no point. I've tried to learn before. I'm just never going to be a performer."

"Not with that attitude, you're not," Frankie said, pulling him down the hallway to the gymnasium, where they'd set up three layers of mats, one atop the other.

"Don't worry." Banjo patted his shoulder. "It's always scarier than it looks."

"We're going to start at the very beginning," said Frankie. "Not with handstands or cartwheels—that's too advanced."

Seb flushed. "Honestly, guys, I—"

Frankie held up a hand for silence. "We're starting with somersaults," she said. "And Banjo and I are going to do them with you."

"It'll be fun," Banjo said. He tucked himself into a ball and demonstrated a forward roll.

"I don't know about that." Seb sighed. He tried to imitate Banjo's roll, but ended up sprawled on the mat.

"Keep your head tucked," said Frankie. "Pretend your chin is glued to your chest."

He did as she said, and tried again. And again. And again.

"You're getting it!" Banjo cheered, rolling beside him.

Seb knew they were just being nice, but somehow it mattered less with them all rolling around together, and no frowning teachers there to watch. Then Frankie invented a game of somersault tag, and for nearly half an hour, they tumbled after each other, shrieking and laughing.

Finally, they collapsed on the mat, too dizzy to move.

"If Basic Acrobatics were like this," Seb had to admit, "I might actually like it."

"You should take over teaching it, Frankie," Banjo giggled.

Seb folded his hands behind his head and looked up at ceiling, just in time to see a flash of crimson in the directrice's office window above. He'd been so caught up in his lesson that he'd forgotten she might be there. He could only imagine what she was thinking as she watched him tumble—if you could call it tumbling—with the bêtes noires.

Then he recalled the third condition of his probation. It was only a matter of time before she asked him about his father's contribution to the school.

He closed his eyes and sighed, wishing Frankie and Banjo could help him with that one too. He didn't have a clue how he would deal with it alone.

SEB CALLED HOME that evening, hoping to get Maxime's help with the situation. But Maxime had other things on his mind. Ticket sales had been poor in Slovakia, he reported, and they didn't expect much better in Poland, their next destination.

"Oh." Seb gulped, putting his own worries aside to focus on the Konstantinovs. "How's everyone feeling?"

"Not great, to be honest. We could really use some goods news around here." He coughed. "How are things going in Montreal?"

"Oh. Well, I haven't learned anything really useful yet," Seb admitted. "But I'm working on it. And I think I've made a few friends." It sounded odd even saying it. Seb had never made any friends outside the Konstantinovs.

"Tell me about them," said Maxime.

"Well, there's Banjo Brady," Seb said, sitting down on the carpet in the common room. "He's from a little town on the West Coast, where his parents own a tree-planting camp. Banjo grew up exploring the forest, learning the names of trees and animals, and setting up slacklines. Do you know what slacklining is, Max?"

"Like tightrope walking, but on a loose line?"

"Yeah. He's really good at it," said Seb. "And then there's Frankie."

"Where's he from?" asked Maxime.

"Frankie's a girl, and she's from Rome. She does parkour." And that, Seb realized, was about the extent of his knowledge of Frankie. Her French assignment had described her parents and three brothers, but not in great detail. What he did know for certain was that she was the kind of person who'd only talk about herself when she was good and ready, and no amount of pestering her would change that. Case in point: Murray's nose.

Maxime coughed again.

"Are you okay, Max?" Seb asked.

"Oh sure," Maxime said, clearing his throat. "There's just a cold going around and I've got a sore throat."

"You should take care of that," Seb advised. A sword swallower needed a healthy throat like an acrobat needed an unfractured metatarsal. "Hot water and lemon," he advised. "That's always worked in the past, right?"

Maxime agreed. "Aunt Tatiana's been trying to feed me garlic too."

"Gross," said Seb. "I hate it when she does that."

Maxime laughed, then began coughing again. "I have to go, Seb. But someone else wants to talk to you."

"Okay, nice talking to you," Seb said.

"You too, Seb," said Maxime. "*Bon courage.*"

He heard the phone being passed. Then, "Heya, kid!" said Stanley. "Hey, did you hear about the fire at the circus?"

"The fire?" Seb sat bolt upright. "No! Max didn't tell me! What happened?"

"Oh man, it was a bad one," said Stanley. "The heat was intense!" He paused, then burst into laughter. Seb could hear him jingling the bells on his shoes. "Get it? *In tents?*"

Seb sank back down, his heart still hammering. "Jeez, Stanley. Don't do that to me."

"Ha ha! Got you there, didn't I?" Stanley hooted. "Aw, I miss having you around, kid."

"Well, that makes one of us," Seb replied gruffly. Though of course it wasn't true. Even if the Konstantinovs were seven shades of bonkers, he still missed each one of them, every day.

17

"**I**'VE GOT A surprise for you guys today," Oliver Grey announced in English class one afternoon the following week.

"More prepositions?" Murray groaned. The trapeze "master" had finally had his bandages removed, and he seemed to be enjoying the sound of his own voice again.

"Not today," Oliver said good-naturedly. "Though I'd be happy to give you some extra homework, Murray. Today we're—" He stopped as the door creaked open, and in slipped Banjo.

"Sorry," Banjo whispered.

"No problem." Oliver gestured for him to sit down. "Everything okay?"

Banjo nodded, but his eyes told Seb everything: the homemade map wasn't working, and Banjo was still getting lost. Now he had only two more weeks to find his internal compass before the directrice shipped him back to Stumpville.

"Don't worry," Seb mouthed to Banjo, though if he were Banjo, he definitely would have been worried. He glanced over at Frankie, who was mauling her pencil, eyes narrowed. Seb was getting to know this look. It meant she was scheming.

"As I was saying," Oliver went on, "today we're going to write stories."

Stories! Seb spun back around to face the front. Murray groaned again.

"Stories about what?" asked Giselle.

"Anything you want," said Oliver. "A teacher of mine once said you should write about whatever haunts you. Not necessarily something scary, but something that's always *there*, at the back of your mind." He tapped the back of his head, where his red curls looked like they hadn't been combed in a few days. "We've all got something there."

Seb didn't even have to ponder it—he knew exactly what he was going to write about. Or rather, what he *had* to write about. He flipped open his notebook, uncapped his pen and began. The words came rushing like water from the drinking fountain that spurted right into your face, and Seb kept his head close to his notebook, trying to capture every one. Before he knew it, the bell was ringing and class was over.

He sat up, dazed. Oliver was telling the class that they'd resume writing the next day, but Seb knew he'd have to continue that night. Possibly by flashlight, once Sylvain was asleep.

"Hey, Seb," Oliver said as he stood up. "Can you stay a few minutes?"

"Me?" said Seb. "Um, okay." Had he done something wrong? he wondered. Maybe he'd checked out too many library books? Or maybe he was being sent to the directrice's office again, to discuss his father's contribution to the school. He gulped.

"You looked pretty intent there," Oliver said once everyone else had left.

"Oh." Seb flushed. "Yeah. I guess . . . I had a lot to write about."

"Do you mind if I read a bit of your story?" Oliver asked. "Feel free to say no," he added. "I'm just curious."

"Oh!" Seb looked down at his notebook, relieved that he wasn't getting sent to the directrice's office. "I guess so. It's just a work in progress, though."

"I'll only read a page or two," Oliver promised.

While his teacher read, Seb pulled out his latest library find, a novel called *Mount Mystery*. It looked like a good story—something about a plane crash in the

Rocky Mountains. But he couldn't stop stealing glances at Oliver, trying to read the teacher's expression while he read Seb's story.

He was beginning to get anxious when Oliver looked up. "This is good, Seb," he said. "Really good."

"Really?" Seb squeaked, then cleared his throat. "I mean, it's just a work in—"

"Progress. I know." Oliver smiled. "But it's very well written. And a great idea: circus animals escaping a zoo and trying to survive in the Romanian countryside. There's lots of potential for conflict, and that's important in a story. Do you know how it's going to end?"

Seb didn't. "Realistically, they probably won't survive in Romania," he told his teacher. "It might not be a happy ending."

Oliver considered this. "It would be challenging. But maybe not impossible. They each have unique skills— maybe they can help each other survive."

"Maybe," Seb said, though he still wasn't sure.

"You know," said Oliver, "I once heard a story about a couple of penguins escaping the zoo here in Montreal. I don't think they got far, but I always thought that would make a great novel, or even a movie. Have you been to the zoo?"

Seb shook his head. "I haven't left Bonaventure since I got here."

Oliver's jaw dropped. "What? You're kidding. You haven't gone out?"

"Nope," said Seb.

"But it's been almost six weeks! And you're in Montreal, one of the greatest cities in the world—in my opinion," he added. "How can you stand it?"

"I am getting a little twitchy," Seb admitted.

"I bet." Oliver shook his head. "Well, look, my point is that this is a great start to a story. I think you're a writer, Seb." He handed him back his notebook.

Seb was startled. "A writer?"

"A good one," Oliver confirmed. "Now, you'd better get going."

Seb gathered his books and left the classroom. "A writer," he repeated to himself. Him. Was Oliver just being nice? He didn't seem like the type to hand out random compliments.

"A writer."

He liked the sound of that.

THE FOLLOWING SATURDAY morning, Seb tucked *Mount Mystery* under his arm and headed down to the student lounge. He chose a couch far away from the phone, where Banjo was talking to Theo and Lily back home, flopped down and got comfortable.

But no sooner had he cracked the novel's spine than Frankie appeared, wearing slippers, flannel pajamas and what looked like three layers of sweaters. A long, woolen scarf was wrapped around her neck.

She sank down beside him on the couch.

"Cold?" He moved his feet to give her absurdly long legs some room.

"Freezing," she replied, tightening her scarf. "Did they turn off the heat this weekend?"

Seb hummed without looking up from his book, hoping she'd take the hint.

"My hands are like ice." She held one out as proof. He declined to test it. She huffed. "Do you think we can light a fire in the fireplace?"

"Doubt it," Seb replied, trying to concentrate.

Frankie harrumphed and shifted on the couch. The springs bounced. Seb forced himself to take deep breaths.

"I'm getting restless," she informed him.

"I couldn't tell," he replied.

"Next weekend is a long weekend here," she continued, ignoring his sarcasm. "Thanksgiving or something. Oliver's going to be our supervisor."

"That's nice," he said, holding up his novel.

"We'll be stuck inside for three days. And I am dying to do some parkour. Outside. I need to get out."

"Hi, guys," said Banjo, joining them. "What are you up to?"

"Reading," Frankie replied. She moved over to make room for Banjo. He sat, and the springs bounced again.

Seb threw up his hands. "Seriously?"

"Am I interrupting?" Banjo asked anxiously. "I'm sorry."

"Don't get mad at Banjo!" Frankie told him.

Seb gave her the stink-eye, but moved over to give the boy room. "Have a seat," he grunted.

"How are things in Stumpville?" Frankie asked.

"Well," said Banjo, eager to share the report. "All the tree planters have left for the winter now. So it's just Theo and Lily in our cabin. And John and Yoko, of course."

"John and Yoko," Seb repeated.

Banjo nodded.

"Like, on the stereo?"

"Oh, I hope not," said Banjo. "They'd probably break it."

Seb looked at Frankie for help, but she was rewrapping her scarf and grumbling about the cold. "The musicians?" he asked Banjo.

"I wouldn't call them musicians," Banjo said. "But sometimes they howl when Theo plays his ukulele."

"Are we talking about dogs?" said Seb.

"Border Collies," Banjo specified.

"Ahhh." Seb sat back, relieved. He'd concluded from Banjo's stories that Theo and Lily were a little eccentric. But communing with a long-dead musician would have been out there, even for them.

"But not just any Border Collies," Banjo went on. "John and Yoko are more than that. I think sometimes animals can be your friends. Even . . . even family." He looked at Seb. "Does that sound silly?"

"Not at all," said Seb, thinking about the Konstantinov animals. "Tell us about them."

As usual, Banjo was happy to talk about home.

Since there was only a handful of other children in Stumpville—not nearly enough to fill a classroom—Theo and Lily had taught Banjo in their little cabin in the woods. And they'd decided early on that Banjo would be in charge of his own learning, deciding each day what he wanted to study. "They called it an 'alternative education,'" Banjo had explained.

He'd chosen to study the forests and mountains surrounding him. So every day, he'd head out to explore, inspecting the towering cedars and observing the creatures living in and on them. Now and then he'd stop to set up his slackline, and practice under the watchful eyes of John and Yoko.

"I knew that if anything bad happened, they'd run for Theo or Lily," Banjo told his friends. "John and Yoko have great internal compasses too, so they can always find home. Although I'm not sure they'd work here in Montreal." He frowned. "Maybe internal compasses only work in the forest?"

"Maybe," Seb said, but he wasn't sure. "We'd need a forest to test that theory."

"We've got a forest," said Frankie.

"Where?" asked Seb.

"In the middle of the city, remember? The one on the mountain Banjo tried to find that first day."

"I still think about that place," Banjo sighed. "But the directrice will never let me go."

Seb agreed—there was no way she'd ever let the bêtes noires out for a field trip.

But someone else might, he realized. Someone who really loved Montreal . . .

"Leave it to me," he told his friends. "I have another idea."

"THIS IS MY favorite neighborhood in Montreal!" Oliver declared as he led Seb, Frankie and Banjo out of a subway station called Mont-Royal the following weekend. "It's called the Plateau. Isn't it great?" He turned in a slow circle, arms open to the shops and cafés and the sidewalks bustling with Sunday shoppers. "I still can't believe you guys haven't toured the city yet."

"I still can't believe you busted us out!" said Frankie, who'd been keeping herself warm by leaping over random objects, like parking meters and small children. "How did you convince the directrice?"

"I live by the principle of 'act now, apologize later,'" Oliver told her.

"So you didn't ask?" Frankie gaped.

"She's in New York City for the long weekend. Who was I to ask?" Oliver smiled innocently. "I did tell the Scout, though. He approved."

Frankie looked at him with new respect. Then she vaulted off a lamppost.

Seb blinked in the afternoon light, still reeling from the subway ride. It had been a long time since he'd been on a subway (which in Montreal was called the "metro"), and Banjo had never ridden one in his life. But Frankie knew them well; she'd shown them both how to read the map of the different underground lines and stops, and she'd made sure Banjo didn't get lost in the dark, brick-lined tunnels. Frankie seemed right at home amongst the city crowds.

Banjo less so. He stuck close to Seb's side, taking in the Plateau with wide eyes. But he was also smiling—in fact, he hadn't stopped since Seb had triumphantly told him that on the long weekend, Oliver was going take them to

Mont Royal, the famous mountain surrounded by a forest in the middle of the city.

"This way." Oliver steered them down a street called rue Saint-Denis. His old green sneakers bounced as he walked, which told Seb that he'd needed the outing as much as anyone. He felt quite proud of himself.

The Plateau was very different from Old Montreal—there were no cobblestones or old, ornate buildings, and the streets were straight and wide and crammed with cafés serving delicious-smelling things like fresh-baked bagels and eggs Benedict. And there were people every-where—waiting in line for Sunday brunch, peering into bookstores and clothing shops, clutching bags of grocer-ies, zipping down the street on bicycles. On one street corner there was even a piano, just standing there, wait-ing to be played. As they watched, a teenaged girl sat down and began to play a slow, sweet melody.

"I've never seen a city like Montreal," Seb remarked.

"It's one of a kind," Oliver agreed. "Now, who wants some *chocolat chaud*?"

"I'm really more of an espresso drinker," said Frankie. "But I'll make an exception."

"You won't regret it." Oliver steered them into a café, and they emerged minutes later with paper cups filled with thick, dark chocolate topped with whipped cream.

"This is amazing," Seb said between slurps.

"As good as espresso?" Oliver asked Frankie.

"Nope," she said, slurping at her whipped cream. "But still good."

"So, where's the mountain?" asked Banjo.

"We're almost there," Oliver promised. "Next stop, Mont Royal!"

The city was spangled in red and gold, like Dragan Konstantinov's favorite tasseled epaulettes. Leaves drifted like paper flames down from gnarled maples, blanketing the alleyways and little street-corner parks. Seb watched Banjo skip along, nearly spilling his *chocolat chaud*, and hoped this trip would restore the boy's internal compass.

"I haven't seen it yet," Banjo said about ten minutes later.

"Must be a small mountain," Frankie commented, pulling her scarf up over her nose.

Banjo gulped down the last of his *chocolat chaud* and tucked the cup into his backpack. "I can't wait," he whispered to Seb. "Mountains and forests just make me feel right, you know? Do you have a place that makes you feel right?"

Seb had never thought about it before. The theater made him feel good. And so did the library—any place with books, really. But he wasn't sure he'd found a place that made him feel the way forests and mountains made Banjo feel. In fact, he'd—

Oliver stopped. Before them, cars and buses zipped by on a big, noisy street. "There it is!" he declared. "Mont Royal!"

"Where?" Banjo asked, looking around.

"Right there." Frankie pointed beyond the busy street to the red and gold trees rising up to greet the blue sky. "That's it—right, Oliver?"

"That's Mont Royal," Oliver confirmed.

Seb looked up at the Mont. In all his years crisscrossing Eastern Europe, he'd seen many mountains. And this was definitely more of a hill.

Looking down at Banjo's face, he could tell the boy agreed. Banjo's mouth wobbled open, then he bit his lip.

"You okay?" Seb whispered.

Banjo swallowed and squared his shoulders. "Yes," he said. And he turned to Oliver and smiled. "Let's go explore."

Seb had to hand it to Banjo—he put on a very brave face. He'd expected towering cedars and quiet, spongy paths; what he got was a gravel track as wide as a road and teeming with joggers, cyclists and children playing tag.

But Banjo led the way to the very top, where they stopped to look out over the rooftops of Montreal and the great shining river beyond, which Oliver informed them was called the Saint Lawrence River, or *le fleuve Saint-Laurent*, in French.

"It's great," said Banjo, and though Seb could tell it wasn't what he'd been looking for, he could also tell he meant it.

"Isn't it?" Oliver sighed happily.

"Let's not go back," said Frankie, loosening her scarves and tilting her face up to the sun.

They lingered there in the sunshine for as long as they could before starting the long journey back to Bonaventure.

18

"**W**HAT DO YOU mean, nothing?" asked Dragan. "Nothing at all?"

"Not really," Seb admitted, sitting down on the carpet with the telephone. It was the morning after the trip to Mont Royal, and since it was a holiday, he'd decided to phone home. "But it's only October."

"It's *already* October," Dragan corrected him. "You should have learned *something* by now that can help us."

"Dad, come on. I just got here," Seb protested. "I've got almost four years left."

"Well, the Konstantinov Family Circus might not," Dragan snapped. "Winter is always our hardest season. You know that."

"Right, but—"

"And this one is particularly bad."

Seb sat up straight. "What's going on?"

"Maxime has a bad case of bronchitis," Dragan grumbled. "He can't even swallow solid food, let alone medieval weapons. We're down one performer."

"Oh no." Seb's stomach pitched. "But I thought it was just a cold."

"It was," said Dragan. "And now it's not."

"Okay." Seb drew a breath. "But he'll get better. Just tell him to eat Aunt Tatiana's garlic."

Dragan said nothing.

"And in the meantime," Seb hurried on, not liking the silence. "Hire a new act, just for now. Maybe another fire breather? No, don't do that," he said on second thought. "How about a snake charmer? It's been ages since we had one of those."

"There's no money," Dragan said simply.

"But we're Konstantinovs," Seb said, forcing a laugh. "We'll fake it 'til we make it!"

"Seb," Dragan said, slowly and seriously. "I think I have to let Maxime go."

"What?" Seb gasped. "No! No, Dad, you can't! He'll get better, I know he will."

"Seb—"

"Just try feeding him the garlic, Dad! *Feed him the garlic!*" He was yelling now, possibly loud enough to wake

Frankie and Banjo upstairs. But he couldn't help it.

"It's more than that," said Dragan. "Sword swallowers have gone out—"

"No, they haven't!" Seb yelled. "They're getting big again. I . . . I heard about it here at school," he added. "They're making a comeback. It's going to be huge." It was a lie and they both knew it, but he had to try.

"Seb," Dragan said softly.

"Not Maxime, Dad," he pleaded. "Not yet. Just . . . just wait until he's better. You can't fire him when he can't swallow solid food."

"I can't wait much longer, Seb," his father told him. Now he didn't sound angry, or even irritated. Just . . . defeated.

Which was far, far worse.

FOR DAYS, SEB could think of little else but his conversation with his father. He searched online for bronchitis remedies and emailed Maxime recipes for homemade throat soothers. But Maxime didn't respond, which only made him more anxious.

It didn't help when he woke on Thursday morning to find a note slipped under his dorm room door. A note written on heavy cardstock, smooth to the touch.

"What's that?" asked Sylvain. He was sitting on the top bunk, swinging his legs over the edge while eating his first breakfast of chocolate-covered marshmallows.

"Not sure," Seb said, unfolding it. But he knew it wasn't good.

Dear Sebastian, the note read. *I can't help but notice that you have not yet contributed to the school as we agreed you would. Would you be so kind as to send me an update? I am too busy to speak with you directly, so please leave a note with my assistant, Bruno.*

Angélique Saint-Germain

Definitely not good.

"What's up?" asked Sylvain. "Is that from *her*?" He jumped down from the top bunk.

"Yeah." Seb quickly pocketed the note. "Just . . . a reminder that I'm on probation."

Sylvain shook his head. "Wow, that's rough. Here, have breakfast." He offered Seb some marshmallows, which Seb declined. Between Maxime's illness and the directrice's surprise note, he was in no mood to eat.

He wasn't the only one out of sorts that morning. Overnight, the hot water heater had broken, leaving all the students stuck with cold showers, just as the temperature outside dipped further.

"I am *freezing*," Frankie grumped on their way to Basic Acrobatics. She'd wrapped herself in scarves, like a woolen mummy. Seb wasn't sure how she was going to do acrobatics like that, but he didn't ask.

When they entered the gymnasium, they found the Scout waiting, dressed as usual in a spotless suit, hair perfectly coiffed.

"Good morning," he greeted them. "I'm standing in for Monsieur Gerard for a bit. All the teachers are in an emergency meeting this morning."

"About what?" asked Sylvain.

"Hopefully it's about who's going to fix the hot water heater," Frankie grumbled.

"Totally," Sylvain agreed, holding up his hand for a high five. But Frankie refused to take her hands out of her pockets, and left him hanging again.

"I'll get on that right away," the Scout promised. "But the teachers have other things to talk about—teacher things, you know."

The students did not know. But it didn't sound terribly interesting, so they let it go and started on their warm-ups.

"Hey, where's Banjo?" Frankie asked as she and Seb stretched their hamstrings side by side.

Seb had been pondering what on earth he would tell the directrice in his update, but now he straightened and looked around. "He's not here?"

"Nope," said Frankie. "Did you see him at breakfast?"

"I skipped breakfast today," Seb said, now very much wishing he hadn't.

Frankie shook her head grimly. "Lost again. I guess that means the field trip didn't work either."

Seb sighed. He'd had high hopes for Mont Royal.

"Well, hopefully he makes it before—"

The door banged open and Monsieur Gerard stomped in. Without a word to the students, he stalked over to the Scout, mustache twitching. The Scout leaned over to listen, then nodded and patted the teacher on the shoulder. Frankie and Seb exchanged eyebrow raises.

"What do you think that's about?" Seb whispered.

"Don't know," murmured Frankie. "But this is a bad day for Banjo to be late."

Moments later, the Scout slipped out, and Monsieur Gerard turned to the students.

"Handstands!" he bellowed, making everyone jump. "Pair up and start practicing! I want to see perfection today!"

The students scattered, and Frankie and Seb headed for the wall.

"Maybe one of us should go find him," Seb whispered when they reached it. "We could tell him to fake sick so he wouldn't get in—"

But then the gymnasium door squeaked open, and in slipped Banjo.

"Trouble," Seb finished.

"Monsieur Brady!" Monsieur Gerard bellowed. "Explain why you are late! Again! *Encore!*"

"I-I-I'm sorry," Banjo stammered. "I just . . . got turned around."

Monsieur Gerard pointed at the wall. "You will sit this class out today, Banjo. And tomorrow you will arrive on time."

"I'm sorry, I—" Banjo began.

Monsieur Gerard drove his finger toward the wall.

Banjo ducked his head and followed it.

"Francesca!" the teacher hollered not five minutes later, as they began their practice. "Your form is completely off. I've never seen you so sloppy! Try again."

Frankie rumbled under her breath but did as she was told.

"*Non! Non!*" Monsieur Gerard tore at his hair. "You are not trying. You are not striving for perfection."

Frankie flipped down from what Seb thought was a perfectly decent handstand. "What's the point?" she asked, righting herself.

"The point?" Monsieur Gerard repeated. "The *point?*"

"Frankie," Seb murmured nervously.

"The point, Mademoiselle de Luca," he yelled, "is excellence! To excel in acrobatics, or any circus skill, you must have discipline. And you lack it *complètement*. You might be a decent freerunner—"

"*Traceur!*" Frankie snapped. "I'm a *traceur*. I do parkour."

The entire gymnasium grew suddenly quiet.

"I don't care what you do," Monsieur Gerard said, his voice now quiet. "Today you will do nothing but sit and watch with Monsieur Brady."

Frankie opened her mouth to protest, then closed it and headed for the wall. Practice resumed.

Seb watched her join Banjo, leaving him to attempt handstands by himself. And suddenly, everything just felt very heavy—Maxime's illness, the state of the Konstantinovs, the directrice's note, the cold showers, his friends on the sidelines. It made his shoulders weak; there was no way he could pull off a handstand.

And so, he joined the bêtes noires.

"You're going to be in so much trouble," Frankie said as he sat down beside her.

"I know." He could feel Monsieur Gerard's glare without even looking at him. "So, what's the difference?"

"Huh?"

"Between freerunning and parkour," he said. "How are they different?"

"Oh. Well, parkour is about getting places, fast," said Frankie. "Freerunning is more about being creative.

Freerunners do lots of tricks, and it's fun to watch—
there's nothing wrong with it. But it's not my thing.
Parkour has a purpose. It's what you need when you're
running for your life—" Suddenly she stopped.

"Wait, *what?*" asked Seb.

"Running for your life?" Banjo whispered.

Frankie shook her head and closed her mouth tight.

"What do you mean?" Seb persisted, but she refused to
say. "Come on, Frankie, you can't just—" he began.

"Silence!" roared Monsieur Gerard. "One more word
and you'll be back in the directrice's office!"

Seb snapped his mouth shut and forced himself not
to say another word. It wouldn't have done any good,
anyway—Frankie's lips were sealed, and he knew she
meant it.

19

MONSIEUR GERARD WASN'T the only teacher out of sorts, it turned out. After the emergency staff meeting, all the teachers at Bonaventure seemed off. The juggling instructor botched a simple behind-the-back toss. The aerials teacher accidentally tied herself in a knot while climbing the silks. And at dinner that night, some third-year students recounted how their unicycle instructor had gotten his pant leg caught in his spokes and tumbled head over wheel.

The following day, things were no better; even Audrey Petit wasn't acting like herself in clown class. Her usual prance was more of a walk, which made her billowy rainbow pants sag.

"Cold in here, isn't it," she remarked, rubbing her arms. The Scout hadn't yet been able to fix the hot water heater.

"Freezing," said Frankie, who'd taken to wearing her clown nose for warmth.

Audrey nodded, then drew a deep breath and forced a smile. "Well, then, we'll just have to get moving! Today we're going to go exploring."

"Outside?" Murray grimaced.

Audrey shook her head. "Right here in school."

"But we've explored the school," Camille pointed out. She, too, had been out of sorts since the previous day, when Monsieur Gerard called her cartwheels "average."

"You've explored it as yourselves," said Audrey. "But you haven't explored it as clowns." She gestured for everyone to gather around her, and they did—for warmth if nothing else.

"The clown lives in the present moment," Audrey told them. "Most of us, especially adults, spend a lot of time thinking about what's coming next, or what just happened, or sometimes what happened a long time ago, and how we could have changed it." Here she looked at Seb, who'd just been pondering what might have happened if he'd never left the Konstantinovs.

He shook his head and tried to focus.

"And that's why clowns can see things differently," Audrey continued. "Audacité will see the same object as I do, but she'll find a different use for it—one that suits her right in that moment." She held up a finger. "Watch."

Audrey popped her red ball onto her nose and began skipping around the class, smiling wide. When she reached Frankie, she stopped and began inspecting her scarf. Frankie drew back, but Audacité persisted, grabbing the scarf and unwinding it from Frankie's neck.

"Hey!" Frankie cried, and a few students giggled. Seb wondered if Audacité had perhaps forgotten the crunch of Frankie's left hook. He hoped she knew what she was doing.

Audacité ignored them all, holding up the scarf and shrieking with delight, like a small child with a new toy. Then she began to play with it, first as a skipping rope, then as a parachute, then a lasso. She swung the lasso, trying to capture Frankie, and eventually, even Frankie laughed.

"You see?" Audrey slipped off her nose. "How your inner clown feels in the moment determines how they see the things around them. If Audacité was feeling sad, she might have used Frankie's scarf as a giant tissue for blowing her nose."

Seb was relieved. That would not have gone well for Audacité.

"Now." Audrey clapped her hands. "We're going to explore the school as clowns. Touch things and smell things and feel things. Find new uses for the objects you encounter, based on how your clown feels in the moment."

The students charged out of the room, and Seb followed. He headed for the library, thinking maybe his inner clown could find a new use for a book. But just as he rounded the corner, Frankie popped out in front of him, red nose peeking out over her scarf. Seb jumped.

"I've got it!" she announced.

"Sorry, what?" he asked, composing himself.

"I've got it," she repeated, pulling off her clown nose. "Believe it or not, this was inspiring."

"You've found your inner clown?"

She shook her head. "I've got an idea for curing Banjo. And it's a good one this time. Not that yours weren't," she added quickly.

Seb shrugged, still a little disappointed that they hadn't worked. "Okay, what's your idea?"

But Frankie shook her head. "Tomorrow morning. In the gym," she said. "I'll explain then." She pulled up her scarf and jogged away.

ON SATURDAY MORNING, Frankie stood before Seb and Banjo, fists on her hips and woolen cap pulled down over her ears. "Okay, you two," she said. "I've made you wait long enough."

"You're killing us, Frankie." Seb sighed. "What are we doing?"

"We're going to explore the school," Frankie announced. "Like we did in clown class!"

"Exploring the school as clowns?" Seb raised an eyebrow. "How is that going to help?" It also sounded like an awful way to spend a Saturday.

"Not as clowns," Frankie corrected him. "We're going to explore as *traceurs.*"

"We're doing parkour?" asked Banjo.

Frankie grinned. "When you become a *traceur,* you start to see your city differently. Instead of roads and sidewalks and signs, you'll see obstacles and ways to get around them. The city becomes a new place, even if you've lived there all your life. I think it could help Banjo get to know the school."

"Okay." Banjo licked his lips. "I'm up for trying it."

"Maybe I'll just watch," said Seb. He wasn't sure Audrey, their supervisor that weekend, would be up for an impromptu trip to the hospital.

"Don't worry," said Frankie. "Parkour is about speed, but also safety. Come on." And she turned and jogged out of the gymnasium. Banjo followed, and Seb took up the rear, wondering what he was getting himself into.

First, Frankie ran to the cafeteria, where she taught

them to jump over chairs and land soundlessly on the balls of their feet.

"No easy feet," Seb quipped.

"Less joking, more jumping," said Frankie. But she was smiling.

Next, she ran to the theater, where she had them climb up onto the stage without using their knees, then leap off and land with a roll to break the fall. Miraculously, the fall was the only thing Seb did break. He credited that to the saints watching over them.

"Thanks, guys." He clapped the statues on the shoulder on his way out, now headed back to the gym. There, Frankie showed them how to tic-tac, or run at a wall and use it as a springboard.

Once they'd learned a few skills, the exploration began. They ran up hallways and down stairwells, springing off walls and hurdling chairs and the odd potted plant. They dove in and out of classrooms, gasping for breath, cheering each other on. Soon Seb stopped thinking about his bad form and the possibility of broken bones. All that mattered was the next turn they'd take and the obstacles they'd find.

Until they heard a voice that sounded like Angélique Saint-Germain.

Frankie ground to a halt, and Seb and Banjo had to fling themselves back to avoid bowling her over. She put her hand up for silence, and they huddled together, listening. Had they imagined it?

Something cold and wet hit Seb square on the head, and he yelped and looked up. Overhead, a pipe was dripping; underfoot, water was pooling fast.

"This is *not* the way Saturdays are meant to be spent."

It was definitely the directrice's voice. And she was headed their way.

"Go! Go!" Frankie shoved the boys toward the nearest door, which was mercifully unlocked. They dove inside just before Angélique Saint-Germain rounded the corner.

"Where are we?" Banjo whispered.

Seb felt around in the darkness until his hand found what felt like a feather boa. "Costume closet," he replied.

Frankie opened the door just a crack so they could all peer out.

"Saturday mornings," Angélique Saint-Germain was saying, "are to be spent reading the newspaper. In slippers. With scones. *Not* fixing leaky pipes."

"Agreed," someone replied, and Seb caught sight of the Scout, wearing jeans and a sweatshirt and brandishing a wrench. "Though I'm more of a cinnamon bun kind of guy," he added.

The directrice was not amused. "I'm just glad you were home when I called," she said. "Bruno is useless when it comes to fixing anything."

"Well, I wouldn't say use—" the Scout began.

"Useless," Angélique Saint-Germain repeated. "Here it is. Can you fix it?"

"I think so," the Scout said, assessing the leaky pipe. "I dabbled in plumbing, years ago."

"Of course he did," muttered Frankie.

The Scout opened a stepladder and climbed up while the directrice watched below, arms crossed. Ennui sank down on the wet carpet, looking like he too was missing his Saturday scones.

"Things are getting dire, Michel," the directrice said.

The Scout removed a ceiling panel and stuck his head into the gap, humming in agreement.

"Pipes to patch, furnaces to fix," she went on. "And where is the money going to come from? *You know who* hasn't made any donations yet."

Seb swallowed. He was fairly certain he knew who.

The Scout made another humming noise that seemed to mean it was indeed a quandary.

"Well, you don't know the half of it," said Madame Saint-Germain. "Remember that boy who fell from the silks last year? What was his name?"

"Daniel?" came the muffled reply.

"That's the one."

"How is he?" The Scout pulled his head out, looking concerned.

"Nothing a little surgery won't fix, I'm sure." She waved at him to continue working.

"That was unfortunate," the Scout said, resuming his work.

"Indeed," said the directrice. "When a student falls from a ripped silk that was too old to use in the first place, it does nothing to improve a school's reputation."

"I meant for his arms," said the Scout.

"Yes, yes, that too." The directrice waved this away. "But now rumor has it his family might be suing us. And that cannot happen, Michel. We're already in the red. *Deeply* in the red."

"In the crimson," whispered Seb.

"What?" said Frankie.

"Nothing."

Ennui lifted his head from his paws and turned to stare at the closet door. Then he heaved himself up and trudged over to it, sniffing deeply.

"Oh no," Seb whispered. "Go away."

Unsurprisingly, the bulldog didn't obey. Instead, he stepped right up to the door and nudged it open with his nose.

"Oh no you don't." Frankie quickly pushed it back and held it there. The dog whined.

"What are you looking at, Henri?" the directrice asked. "What's in there?"

The bêtes noires held their breath.

"Probably a rat," the Scout said, pulling his head out of the gap in the ceiling tiles. "I saw one in the janitor's closet the other day."

"Gross," whispered Frankie.

The directrice shuddered. "That's exactly my point. This place needs fixing, which means we must cut costs elsewhere." She gestured for him to keep working, and he stuck his head back in the gap. "The teachers won't take it well, as we saw at the emergency staff meeting. But it's necessary. Some of them will have to lose their jobs."

"Where will you start?" the Scout asked, sounding a bit wary.

"I'm thinking with Bruno," she said.

He motioned for her to pass him the wrench. "Is that really necessary?"

"I need to start somewhere," she said, passing it. "And Bruno is fairly useless."

"But then you won't have an assistant," the Scout pointed out. "You'll have to answer your own phone calls."

The directrice shuddered again. "Good point. Perhaps I'll keep him a while longer and get rid of the juggling teacher. You know how I feel about jugglers."

The Scout hummed in response, and the pipe stopped dripping.

"The other option," Angélique Saint-Germain said, bending to pick up Ennui, "is to get rid of a few students. Just a few. The ones we know will never be world-class performers."

"Uh-oh," Frankie whispered.

The Scout retreated down the ladder, then wiped his hands on his jeans. "Which students do you have in mind?" he asked, now sounding very wary.

"You know exactly which ones," she replied. "The bêtes noires."

Seb, Frankie and Banjo gulped.

"I still don't know what you were thinking, recruiting them in the first place," the directrice said. "That Banjo from Stumptown? He hasn't made it to a class on time yet."

"Stumpville," Banjo croaked. They hushed him.

"And the de Luca delinquent? There's something you're not telling me about that one, isn't there, Michel?"

Frankie sucked in her breath.

"Frankie is a talented *traceur*—" the Scout insisted.

"And the Konstantinov boy!" the directrice went on. "No skills, no charisma *and* he tells absurd lies! What were you thinking?"

"Well, his father—"

"His father. Exactly." She stabbed the air with a finger.

"That's the only reason I haven't shipped the boy back to Moldova, or wherever. I'm still holding out hope for Dragan's money. Though I have to say, I'm quickly losing patience. Sebastian hasn't even replied to my note. It's a bad sign, Michel."

"What note?" Banjo whispered. Seb shook his head.

"Angélique," said the Scout. "Please give them a bit more time. I know it's hard to see, but each one of them shows promise. Even Seb."

The directrice frowned. Seb cringed down to his toes.

"Just until spring," the Scout insisted. "And in the meantime, we'll think of other potential donors. Come on, let's go put our heads together. I'll buy you a scone." He steered her away, and Ennui gave the closet door one last glare, then trudged after them.

Once they were long gone, Frankie pushed open the door, and they all crawled out.

"This is bad, isn't it," Banjo said, shaking sequins from his hair.

"Really bad," Frankie confirmed. Seb nodded, feeling ill.

"If I get sent home, Theo and Lily will be so disappointed," said Banjo. "They said this was the most alternative of alternative educations. They were so excited for me." He chewed on his lower lip. "I can't let them down."

"If I get sent home," Frankie began, then stopped. "Well, I *can't* get sent home. I just can't."

And if I get sent home, Seb thought, there's no one left to save the Konstantinov Family Circus.

"I can't either," he said.

"So what can we do?" asked Banjo.

"It sounds like the only thing that's going to save us— and the Bonaventure Circus School—is money," said Frankie.

Seb thought for a moment. He was having a hard enough time saving his own circus from the crimson— scrounging up money for Bonaventure wasn't really an option. "Maybe all we can do for now is try not to get noticed," he said. "We need to stay out of trouble."

Frankie nodded. "Good point. We'll have to fly under the radar."

"We can do that," said Banjo. "I think."

"We'll be stealthy, like ninjas," Frankie said.

"We'll blend in," added Banjo. "Like stinkbugs."

"Stinkbugs?" Seb repeated.

Banjo nodded. "Camouflage. They're really good at it."

"Stinkbugs. Okay," said Seb. "We'll try, anyway." Though considering their track record thus far, it wouldn't be easy.

20

AND SO THEY tried to fly under the radar, stealthy like ninjas and camouflaged like stinkbugs. Frankie took time each day to work on her French, usually with Seb's help. And in Basic Acrobatics, she focused on clean lines and stopped questioning the point of it all (at least out loud).

Seb was still terrible at circus skills. But he practiced, every Saturday and Sunday afternoon, alongside Banjo and Frankie. He tumbled and cartwheeled, worked on his three-ball cascade, and even tried to build some muscle lifting the smallest dumbbells he could find in the gym.

He also wrote the directrice a note, saying that Dragan was very busy planning a new show but would be happy to discuss a contribution in the spring. He dropped it off at Bruno's tiny desk and hurried away before the man could read it. He hoped very much that one of these days the only stories he'd have to make up would be for English class.

Banjo, meanwhile, began to set his alarm clock half an hour early, to give himself more time to get to Basic Acrobatics. Frankie and Seb did their best to shepherd him from one class to another, and some evenings he even studied his homemade map.

Then one day, about two weeks after that fateful morning in the costume closet, Seb and Frankie arrived at English class only to realize that Banjo was missing. Again.

"Didn't you have lunch with him?" Frankie asked Seb.

Seb nodded. "But he had to go back to his room after."

"And you let him go *alone?*" Frankie looked at him incredulously.

"I had to go to the library!" Seb protested. "And anyway, where were *you?*"

But Frankie didn't answer, for she was staring at something behind Seb.

"What?" he turned around, then gasped.

Banjo had walked into the classroom. By himself. On time.

"You made it!" they cried as he bounded over gleefully.

"I know, right?" Banjo grinned. "I can't even explain it. For some reason it just made sense today. Maybe it was the parkour—or the map," he added quickly, nodding at Seb.

Frankie beamed like a proud parent. Seb didn't even care whose idea had worked best in the end. All that mattered was that Banjo's internal compass had returned, and with no time to spare, for his month-long probation was almost over.

And so October ended, and the directrice didn't come to collect them and ship them back to Stumpville, Rome or Moldova. But they didn't let themselves get too comfortable, for there was still an air of great unease at Bonaventure, especially among the teachers.

Under the radar they flew, through November as the temperature dropped further, and into December when the snow began to pile up on the rooftops outside. By this point, they'd all concluded that staying out of trouble was surprisingly exhausting.

"My brain hurts," Frankie moaned one evening in mid-December as she flopped down beside Seb on a couch in the student lounge. "But look." She tugged a crumpled piece of paper out of her pocket and handed it to him.

He smoothed it out. It was a French verb test, written in Frankie's scribbles. At the top of the page was a big red "B."

"Frankie!" He gaped. "You passed!"

"Sure did." She grinned. "Thanks to you."

"Well." Seb blushed. "It was a team effort." And they

shook hands proudly before slouching back on the couch, exhausted by their efforts.

Across the room, Banjo was talking on the phone to his parents, which he still did at least three times a week. Seb, on the other hand, barely managed a weekly call home, and when he did, his father was usually too busy to talk. This did nothing to quell Seb's nerves. He knew Maxime was still with the Konstantinovs, and according to Stanley he could once again eat solid food. But Seb knew better than to assume that things had improved.

When Banjo finished his call, he flopped down beside his friends with a big sigh.

Frankie and Seb exchanged a look. Banjo wasn't one for *ennui*. They sat up straight.

"And how are things in Stumptown, Monsieur Brady?" Frankie asked, rolling her Rs à la Angélique Saint-Germain.

"Stumpville," Banjo sighed, missing the joke. "It wasn't the best year in our camp. We broke even, but not by much. So Theo and Lily can't fly me home for the solstice like they'd wanted to."

"That's too bad," said Seb. "But, um, what's a solstice?"

"You don't know?" Banjo looked incredulous.

Seb shook his head and looked at Frankie, who shrugged.

"It's only the best day of the whole year!" Banjo

exclaimed. "The darkest and the shortest day—the first day of winter!"

"Sounds delightful," said Frankie. She grabbed a deck of cards from a nearby table and began shuffling them.

"It is," said Banjo. "Theo and Lily have never been big on Christmas, so we celebrate the winter solstice instead."

"My family's big on Christmas," Frankie said.

Seb looked at her in surprise; she still almost never mentioned her life back in Rome. He waited quietly for her to continue.

"When I was little," she recalled, "all the de Lucas would get together on the *vigilia*, the night before Christmas, at my uncle Raphael's house. It was big and fancy, so we'd have to wear our best clothes. My brothers and I hated that—especially Aldo, who can't eat without spilling everything. But it was always worth it for the food. Thirteen courses." She closed her eyes and smiled. "Of fish."

"Thirteen?" Banjo was incredulous.

"Fish?" Seb made a face, then quickly erased it when Frankie glared at him. "Sorry. Go on."

"The fried eel was my favorite," she said. "But that was before everything changed. We still have a *vigilia* meal, but it's just in our apartment. Which is good for Aldo, since he can spill all he wants. But I miss the eel."

"What happened that changed everything?" Seb asked.

She shuffled the cards again, like a seasoned poker dealer. "Long story," she said. "Anyway, I won't be going home either this year. How about you?" she asked Seb.

"There's no time to fly all the way to Eastern Europe," he said, though there was, really—they had two entire weeks off. What there wasn't, however, was money. None of the Konstantinovs had even suggested he come home for the holidays.

"Will you miss it?" Banjo asked.

Seb considered this, then nodded. "At Christmas we always park the caravans for a few days and have our own celebration. Aunt Tatiana makes giant vats of goulash and huge trays of gingerbread, and everyone performs for each other, but not their usual acts. Just in whatever way makes them happy."

Like Frankie, he closed his eyes to picture it—the flaming juggling pins arcing into the night sky, the aerialist climbing as high on the silks as she dared, then letting herself tumble toward the ground, her expert knots catching her right before she crashed. Toward the end of the night, the acrobats would form a human Christmas tree, and someone would wrap Seb in a shiny gold silk. Then he'd get hauled up, passed hand over hand until he reached the very top—the star at the top of the tree. He always protested, since it was terrifying being that high up. But it was also electrifying—the only time of year he got to shine.

This year would be nothing like that, and he tried not to feel sad about it. At least he'd have Frankie and Banjo around, and lots of time to read. Also, he soon found out that Oliver Grey would be their supervisor.

"You don't spend the holidays with your family?" he asked Oliver after English on one of their last days of class before the holidays.

"Nah," said Oliver. "My family likes to go to Florida, and I think Christmas should be spent in the cold and snow."

Seb was glad Frankie wasn't around. She'd certainly have something to say to that.

"Speaking of holidays . . ." Oliver shuffled through some papers and pulled out a particularly rumpled one. "I wrote down the titles of some circus shows I think you'll like. You can watch them all online during the break, when you've got some time off."

"What kind of circus shows?" Seb asked, taking the paper.

He must have looked skeptical, because Oliver said, "Trust me, you'll like them. They tell great stories."

Seb looked up. "Stories? Really?" He'd given up on ever seeing such a show again.

Oliver nodded. "Let me know what you think. We can talk about them."

Seb left the classroom clutching the list. It wouldn't be Christmas with the Konstantinovs, but maybe it would be okay. Especially with Oliver and the bêtes noires around.

Then an idea popped to mind, and he turned and hurried back.

"Hey, Oliver, would you be able to take us out over the holidays?" he asked. "To explore Montreal again?"

"Oh." Oliver hesitated. "I'd like to, Seb, but I'll have to check this time." He glanced toward the door and lowered his voice. "My 'act now, apologize later' motto didn't go over so well back in October."

"You got in trouble?" Seb exclaimed. "Really? I'm sorry."

"Not your fault," Oliver told him. "It's just that things are tense here these days."

"Yeah." Seb remembered the directrice's plan to cut jobs. She hadn't done it yet, but that didn't mean she wouldn't. "Well, don't worry about taking us out again."

"It's a good idea, though," said Oliver. "And you definitely deserve it, being cooped up here for so long. Also, Montreal is amazing at Christmastime. We could go see some lights, maybe the ice sculptures . . ." Oliver stroked his beard, liberating a few crumbs. "Let me see what I can do. Even our directrice has to have some holiday spirit, right?"

Seb wasn't so sure about this, but he nodded.

"Any idea when you'd like to go?" asked Oliver.

"Well," said Seb, "when is the solstice?"

★ ★ ★

POSSIBLY THE DIRECTRICE really did have some holiday spirit, but more likely the Scout worked his usual magic. Either way, Seb, Frankie and Banjo left Bonaventure for the second time on the shortest and darkest day of the year. Oliver had found them all warm coats that more or less fit, for which Seb was grateful. Frankie was wearing so many layers, he wasn't sure how she could even move, but she went gamely along, picking her way through the snowbanks, as eager as anyone to escape.

Banjo was the most excited. "It almost never snows in Stumpville!" he declared, staring up at the massive flakes hurtling down from a plum-colored sky. "And when it does, it always melts right away." He tried to catch a snowflake on his tongue, but it landed in his eye instead.

"It's perfect for snowballs." Seb formed one in his mitten and tossed it at Frankie. Within moments, an all-out battle ensued.

Once they were all suitably snow-covered, Oliver led them through the streets of Old Montreal to a square strung with thousands of white lights. There was a choir singing carols and people selling steaming cider and roasted chestnuts. And in the middle of the square stood a series of sculptures—a tree, a bear, a giant star—all made of ice and illuminated by blue and purple lights.

"This was the best idea," Banjo whispered to Seb, who nodded, pleased.

Eventually, they agreed it was time for *chocolat chaud*, and Oliver led them to a café packed with people chatting merrily at tables around a fireplace.

"Oh, hey," said Oliver. "I see a few friends over there. I'm going to say hello. You don't mind sitting by yourselves, do you?"

Of course they didn't—sitting by themselves in a café in Montreal felt very grown-up. Oliver gave them some coins for their drinks, then bounced over to see his friends.

They bought big, steaming mugs of *chocolat chaud* and claimed a spot near the fireplace. Frankie settled into a red armchair, peeling off her scarves and hat for the first time in over a month. Seb and Banjo sank onto a couch opposite her.

"So." Seb sipped his *chocolat*. "How should we celebrate the solstice, Banjo?"

"Well." Banjo wiped a dab of whipped cream off his nose. "At home, we light lots of candles. And we make a big meal, with tofu trifle for dessert, and eat by the fire. Sometimes Theo and Lily invite friends, but usually it's just the three of us, and John and Yoko, of course." He thought for a moment. "And we tell stories. Theo always tells the one about how he met Lily, even though we all know it by heart."

It didn't sound like the most riveting story, but Seb encouraged him to tell it anyway. The solstice seemed like a time to be generous.

"Okay." Banjo licked his lips. "First, you should know that in Stumpville, there are two kinds of people. There are tree planters, and there are loggers. And they don't usually get along. It's always been like that." He paused a moment. "So, it was the beginning of summer, maybe thirteen years ago. And Theo had just arrived in Stumpville for his first season of planting. He didn't have an internal compass yet, since he'd never been to the coast. And he ended up wandering away from his team and getting lost in the forest.

"He'd been walking for over an hour when he found himself in a clear-cut—that's a place where all the trees have been chopped down. He was about to turn back when he saw a big black bear lumbering toward him."

"Whoa," Seb breathed. The only bears he'd ever seen were the dancing variety.

"He didn't know what to do," Banjo went on. "He couldn't remember if you were supposed to play dead or climb a tree when you met a bear, so he figured he'd just pick one. And he was about to throw himself in the dirt when he heard a rustling behind him, then felt a hand on his shoulder. And he looked back and saw a woman with a chain saw."

Frankie and Seb gasped.

"She was a logger, and not one bit afraid. She waved her chain saw at the bear and told it to go back where it came from. And you know what? The bear turned right around and left."

"It didn't!" cried Frankie.

"Did," said Banjo. "The woman had grown up on the coast and knew all about bears. So she was about to teach Theo what to do next time he met one. But then she got a good look at him, and he looked at her. And that was it— my parents fell in love, right there in the clear-cut."

"But they were from two different camps," Frankie pointed out.

Banjo nodded. "But their chakras were aligned, so it all worked out."

"What does that mean?" asked Seb.

"True love," Banjo said simply.

Seb had to admit, it was a good story, though if he were telling it, he would have drawn out the scene with the bear. He decided to write it all down later, when he got back to his room.

"Your turn," Banjo told him. "Tell us a story about the circus."

Seb considered several before settling on one about the time a pair of rabbits went missing, only to be found two days later sleeping in Aunt Tatiana's bed, nesting in her beard.

But he'd only just started it when he had to stop. For there was something else he wanted to tell, very badly. And solstice seemed like a time to be honest with people you could trust.

"This isn't a story exactly," he said. "Well, I guess it is. But . . ." He took a breath and proceeded to tell them the truth about the Konstantinov Family Circus, and how he'd come to Bonaventure in hopes of saving it.

"That's why I can't get sent home," he finished. "They're counting on me."

"Wow," Banjo said, looking a little dazed. "And the directrice still expects your dad to donate to the school?"

Seb nodded.

"But he's in the crimson," said Frankie.

"Exactly. And if she finds out, that'll be it for me."

"We won't tell," Banjo promised.

"Thanks," said Seb, feeling suddenly lighter. "I would have told you sooner, but—"

"It's a family secret," Frankie finished. "The kind of thing you keep to yourself." She paused. "Or maybe tell two people you really trust."

Seb looked at her expectantly, wondering if now she would too.

For a few moments, she stayed quiet, sipping her *chocolat chaud*. Then she kicked off her boots and pulled her feet up onto the armchair. "So, it was the night of Cousin

Luigi's wedding," she began. "And I was about nine years old."

Cousin Luigi, it turned out, was the son of Frankie's uncle Raphael, brother to her father, Rocco. Raphael was the one who'd hosted the Christmas parties in his enormous mansion, which he'd built with the fortune he'd earned selling Italy's most sought-after soup.

"Soup?" Seb interrupted, just to be sure he'd heard correctly.

"Minestrone," Frankie specified. "The most delicious minestrone in all of Italy."

Up until that fateful night, all the de Lucas had shared evenly in the soup spoils, for Raphael was a generous man. Frankie's family spent summers in Croatia and could send Frankie and her brothers to a pricey private school. But at Luigi's wedding, just as the guests were digging into their tiramisu, it was revealed that another one of Rocco's brothers had leaked the secret soup recipe to a rival company.

Tempers flared, insults volleyed and a pistol emerged from a suit jacket. Fortunately, Uncle Raphael had terrible aim, and the traitor lost only his left ear for the crime. Unfortunately, Raphael decided then and there to cut his entire family off from his minestrone millions. And Frankie's parents were suddenly left scrambling for money.

"Wow," said Seb. Now *this* was a story.

"So what did they do?" asked Banjo.

"The only thing they could," said Frankie. "They started selling popes."

"Popes?" Seb repeated.

"Popes," Frankie confirmed.

Every week, Rocco de Luca would go out and buy a box of little plaster pope figurines. Then his wife, Rosa, would spread them out on the floor of their little apartment and set to work painting them. But Rosa wasn't a practiced artist, and she didn't have the steadiest hand, so a lot of her popes turned out looking like they'd eaten some bad shellfish.

"My dad said that was the beauty of it," said Frankie. "No pope can live forever, so it's best to have a figurine that doesn't really look like the current one. He said it made for a timeless souvenir."

That sounded like Dragan-type logic. "And he sold enough of them?" Seb asked dubiously.

"Not really," said Frankie. "My brothers and I had to . . . help out." She paused for another long moment. "So we picked pockets in the piazzas."

Seb's mouth fell open.

"We got pretty good at it," Frankie went on. "Tito would grab the wallet or purse, then pass it to me while Aldo caused a distraction—rustling up some pigeons, or faking an injury. Sometimes we'd bring little Pio along to stage a tantrum. Pio has the best tantrums." Frankie smiled. "And then I'd take the prize and run."

"Using your parkour skills!" said Banjo.

Frankie nodded. "And that's how I met the Scout. I stole his wallet."

"You didn't!" Seb gaped.

"I did. But I didn't know he'd dabbled in parkour. I thought I'd lost him, but he followed me up onto a rooftop, and there was nowhere to go. He told me he wouldn't turn me in if I signed up for circus school. I'd already had a few warnings from the *polizia*, so . . ." She sipped her *chocolat* and shrugged.

"That's . . . amazing," said Banjo.

"One of the best stories I've ever heard," said Seb. It also explained a lot—like why her French was riddled with curse words, and why she couldn't get sent home.

"Hey, you three!" Oliver appeared beside them. "We should probably head back now."

"Already?" they groaned, but Oliver stood firm. Reluctantly, they set down their mugs and shuffled back into their coats. But as they headed toward the door, Frankie pulled them both back. "You won't tell anyone, will you?" she whispered. "Even the Scout promised not to."

"Never," said Seb. "If you guys keep my secret too."

They shook on it with mittened hands, then stepped back out onto the snowy street and headed home, their bellies warm with *chocolat chaud* and their heads swimming with stories.

Part 4

JEAN-LOUP

21

SEB SPENT MUCH of the holidays by the fireplace in the student lounge, reading or playing cards with Frankie and Banjo. If he wasn't there, he was in Oliver's office, discussing the shows his teacher had recommended he watch.

"So what'd you think about Rapunzel?" Oliver asked one afternoon. He had kicked off his sneakers and propped his stocking feet up on his desk.

"Pretty good," Seb replied. In that one, a tightrope-walking Rapunzel had been stuck on a high-wire rather than in a tower. Her prince was an aerialist—except he'd had to climb a very long blond wig instead of his usual silks. "It was fun to watch. There were a few weird ones on that list, though," he added. "Like the one with the people wearing antlers and walking around on their hands?" He shook his head. "I don't think I understood that one."

Oliver laughed and tipped back in his chair. "Yeah, that was a weird one. But that's kind of the beauty of the modern circus. It can be so many different things."

Seb nodded. "So do you think a good story makes a good circus show?"

Oliver considered this. "Personally, my favorite shows are the ones that tell stories," he said. "The ones that aren't just about skills, but also plot and character—the things we always talk about in English class."

"Right," Seb said. "Those are my favorites too." It was heartening to know Oliver felt the same, even if Angélique Saint-Germain didn't. He wanted very badly to tell Oliver about the Konstantinov Family Circus, and how he was fairly certain he could save it with some fresh, new shows. But he couldn't—even if Oliver was almost a friend, he was still a teacher at Bonaventure. It was too risky.

"You know, Seb," Oliver said, "I think you'd be really good at writing circus shows."

"Me?" Seb hadn't expected this. "Oh, I don't think so."

"I do," said Oliver. "You're a good writer, and you under-stand all the skills performers can use to tell a story."

Seb wasn't convinced: he barely knew how to write normal stories, let alone stories for circus performers. "I wouldn't know where to start."

"Start with one you've been writing," said Oliver. "You have a few in progress, don't you?"

Seb nodded. "I don't know if they'd make good shows, though."

"Don't overthink it," Oliver advised. "Just try it for fun. This is one case where we're not striving for perfection," he added with a grin.

This made Seb feel a bit better, and he started writing his first circus show that night, after Frankie and Banjo had gone upstairs to bed. He chose the story he knew the best—the one about the animals escaping the zoo, which he'd tentatively titled *The Great Adventure*. And he tried to write it out like a play, but with circus performers expressing themselves through basic acrobatics.

It was hard work—very hard, in fact. Right up there with trying to master a handstand. But this kind of hard work left him feeling excited rather than exhausted. Most of the time, anyway.

"What's wrong?" Banjo asked one day toward the end of the holidays. He and Frankie were playing cards while Seb tackled a particularly challenging scene.

Seb looked up from his notebook. "What do you mean?"

"You're making faces," said Frankie. She furrowed her brow and bared her teeth.

Banjo nodded. "Like that."

"Oh." Seb rubbed his forehead. "I'm just a little stuck. I can't picture how performers would act this out."

"Can we help?" asked Banjo.

"Oh, no," Seb said quickly. "This is just a work in progress. You don't want to see it yet."

Frankie rolled her eyes. "We don't want a performance. Let us help. Strength in numbers, remember?"

Seb frowned. "I don't know."

"Come on." Frankie jumped up. "It'll be fun. Tell us what to do."

"Okay." Seb sighed. "Um, Frankie, pretend you're a lion."

"Easy." Frankie crouched low to the ground.

"And Banjo, you'll be a monkey."

"I've always wanted to be a monkey." Banjo looked pleased.

"And you're on a city street for the first time in your lives."

Banjo and Frankie did as they were told, dodging pretend cars and hiding in imaginary shadows. He'd give them instructions, like when to tumble or jump, and they'd show him what it looked like. Sometimes they even added their own moves—Frankie, of course, had the lion doing parkour within minutes. But it helped, very much so. Within an hour, Seb had a pretty solid scene.

"That was fun!" Banjo said afterward, collapsing on a couch. "Where did you get the idea for that show?"

"From real life," Seb admitted. "Well, sort of." And he told them about the day he'd awoken to find all the animals gone.

"Wow." Banjo shook his head in wonder. "That's some story."

"A story inspired by real life," Frankie added. "Those are the best kind."

Seb agreed. And it gave him an idea for his next show.

AS COZY AND quiet as the holidays were, Seb found himself looking forward to the new semester, or at least to having a few more people around. And judging by the other students' faces when they returned to Bonaventure in January, they were happy to be back as well.

"Does everyone seem a little, I don't know, brighter to you?" Banjo asked as he, Seb and Frankie stretched side by side in their first Basic Acrobatics class of the new year.

"That's because some of us took a two-week-long nap," Sylvain said, plopping down beside them.

"And because we're halfway to summer," added Frankie.

"Yes!" Sylvain held up his hand for a high five. This time, Frankie actually slapped it.

But it was more than that, Seb decided, looking around. Several students were whispering excitedly, even with Monsieur Gerard there, overseeing their stretches. Actually, he realized, even Monsieur Gerard looked excited. Was . . . was he smiling? Seb blinked. The ends of his mustache were definitely perked up.

"Weird," he said. "Something's up."

"Of course it is." Camille sat down with them, flushed and breathless. "Haven't you heard?"

"Heard what?" asked Seb.

"He's coming!" she squealed.

"Who's coming?" asked Banjo.

"Everyone!" Monsieur Gerard clapped his hands. "Our directrice has requested our presence in the theater for a special announcement. Come, we mustn't keep her waiting." He gestured to the door, and his face split into an actual smile.

"Oh, that is just creepy," Frankie whispered.

Seb agreed. He also couldn't help but remember the last time the directrice had interrupted Basic Acrobatics for a special presentation. He hoped this one had nothing to do with unmasking a bête noire.

They filed out of the gym and down the hallway with the other students. In the theater, they grabbed three seats together, among the other first-years.

Just as she had four months before, Angélique Saint-Germain marched out onstage, gripped the microphone and gestured for quiet.

"Clearly, some of you have heard the rumors," she began. "And I can confirm them to be true. We will soon have a very special visitor at our school." She flashed a smile so bright it made Seb wince. "Jean-Loup is coming."

For a moment everyone was silent, then the students erupted into gasps and squeals.

This time, Seb recognized the name straight away. "He *is*?"

"Who's that?" asked Banjo.

"Wait, doesn't *loup* mean wolf in French?" Frankie asked. "A wolf is coming?"

"I met a wolf once," Banjo recalled. "In the forest. They're not as scary as everyone thinks, but I wouldn't want to face one without John and Yoko."

Seb shook his head. "Jean-Loup is a person."

In front of them, Giselle turned around. "Not just any person," she clarified. "The most important person in the circus world."

"What's so great about him?" asked Frankie.

"He has a big circus company called Terra Incognito," Seb told her. "They stage performances in far-off places—"

"Like on a high-wire strung across the Grand Canyon!" Giselle burst in.

"And on the roof of the Leaning Tower of Pisa!" added Camille.

"Right," said Seb. There had been a Terra Incognito show among those Oliver had recommended for him—a daring trampoline act set atop a New York City sky-scraper. It was a first-rate performance, but there hadn't been a story, which had left Seb a bit disappointed.

"He's got a ton of money," Sylvain added. "Also a monocle." He held up his finger in a circle around one eye.

"Huh," said Frankie. "You'd think if he's so rich he could afford real glasses."

Camille and Giselle gave her exasperated looks.

"Quiet, everyone!" the directrice called, and the students obeyed. "I'm glad you all understand how important this is. It's a momentous occasion. A once-in-a-lifetime experience. A man like Jean-Loup never takes time out of his extremely busy schedule to visit a school. I, however, have a personal connection—"

"I heard he was madly in love with her," Camille hissed.

"But she left him at the altar!" added Giselle.

"Oh, stop." Frankie rolled her eyes.

"Actually, that might be true," Seb whispered, recalling Dragan's story. "But I'm not sure about the altar part."

In any case, he had to see the man who'd trumped his father for the directrice's affections.

"Jean-Loup will be arriving very soon," the directrice went on. "This Friday, in fact. He'll begin by touring the school, and it is absolutely critical we make a good impression. An excellent impression," she added. "*Flawless*, even."

"Oh." Seb nodded, suddenly understanding. He lowered his voice and leaned toward Frankie and Banjo. "She must want Jean-Loup to help the school."

"Would he do that?" said Banjo. "Oh, do you think he'll fix the hot water heater?"

"He'd better," grumbled Frankie. "If I have to take one more cold shower I'm going to go insane."

"I mean, she wants him to donate money," said Seb.

"We'll be giving Jean-Loup a tour of the school, and also hosting a Friday night soiree in his honor," the directrice went on. "Of course, no students will be invited, except a select few who will perform."

The students moaned. Seb, Frankie and Banjo, however, exchanged a quick glance.

"Not invited," Frankie murmured. "But not technically forbidden."

"Now, now." The directrice raised a finger. "Lest you think you will not be involved at all, fear not. Here at Bonaventure, we are like family, aren't we? We share in the school's successes and wallow together in its failures."

She smiled at them again, teeth gleaming under the stage lights. "I assure you, each one of you will play an important role in the momentous visit of Jean-Loup."

★ ★ ★

"THIS WASN'T EXACTLY the role I was hoping for," Camille said as she dipped a rag into a bucket of scalding water, then used it to scrub the cafeteria wall.

Beside her, Giselle sighed. "I thought we'd get to give Jean-Loup a tour."

"Yeah, right," said Frankie. "Also, you two need to stop complaining."

Camille and Giselle looked over at the cafeteria table where the bêtes noires were stationed, picking hardened wads of gum off the underside. The twins resumed scrubbing the wall.

It was the day after the big announcement, and the directrice had canceled all classes in preparation for Jean-Loup's arrival. No one at Bonaventure was excused—even the teachers had been put to work patching leaks and mending rips in the carpets. Meanwhile, the directrice patrolled the halls, Ennui at her side, surveying progress.

"I can't believe we got stuck with the gum," Frankie grunted, chipping at a pinkish wad that looked as if it had been stuck there for decades.

"Makes sense to me," grumbled Seb. Who else would Angélique Saint-Germain choose to do the dirtiest work? He hacked at a mottled green piece, which popped off the table and hit him square in the face. "Gross."

"I have a question," said Banjo.

"Shoot." Seb wiped his face with his sleeve.

"Jean-Loup has money, right?"

"More money than God," he confirmed, quoting Dragan.

"And the directrice wants to show him that Bonaventure needs his money, right?"

"I think so."

"So wouldn't it be better to leave everything as it is— dirty and falling apart?" Banjo asked.

Seb and Frankie stopped chipping. Banjo had a point.

"But I'm not going to be the one to suggest it." Frankie resumed her fight with the gum.

"Less talk!" Angélique Saint-Germain commanded from the cafeteria door. "If you're talking, you're not cleaning!"

"*Oui, Madame*," all the students in the cafeteria chorused, picking up the pace.

"She's even scarier than usual today," Sylvain observed once she had left. He was touching up the paint on the baseboards.

"She's stressed," Giselle told him. "J-Loup is a huge deal. That's what his fans call him," she added. Then she grabbed Camille's arm. "We should get monocles for his visit!"

Sylvain snorted.

"He'll never see them," Camille told her. "J-Loup doesn't arrive until after we leave on Friday. They'll give him a tour, put on the show and then he'll be gone forever." She pouted. "The only students who'll see him are the ones chosen to perform."

Again, the bêtes noires exchanged a glance. The promise of watching the show—and Jean-Loup himself—from their hiding spot was the only thing getting them through the preparations.

"They're so lucky," said Giselle, wiping what looked like ancient spaghetti sauce off the wall.

"I don't know about that," said Sylvain. "Marie-Eve was one of the chosen ones, and she hasn't stopped practicing on the tightrope for two days. Her friends have to bring her meals to the gym because the directrice won't let her leave."

"That's not true!" said Camille.

"That's the rumor." Sylvain shrugged. "And I believe it. Can you imagine what she'd do if a student were to mess up in front of J-Loup?" He slashed his paintbrush across his throat. It left a white streak. "Oops," he said.

"What will happen if the school doesn't make a good impression?" asked Banjo.

"An excellent impression," Frankie corrected him. "Flawless, even."

Sylvain snickered. The twins hushed them.

"Jean-Loup could tell the whole circus world that Bonaventure is a bad school. It would hurt our reputation," said Giselle.

"And the directrice's," Seb added.

"Plus, it could ruin the school's chances of getting funding," said Frankie.

"So if Jean-Loup doesn't like the school," Banjo said slowly, "we might all have to go home."

They fell silent. Banjo was right.

Frankie cursed in Italian under her breath.

"That can't happen," Camille proclaimed. For once, Seb agreed with her wholeheartedly.

"I'm not seeing progress!" the directrice bellowed from the doorway, making them all jump. "Scrub! Chip! Paint!"

"*Oui, Madame,*" they chorused. And they got back to work, scrubbing, chipping and painting harder than ever.

22

ON FRIDAY AFTERNOON, all the weekday students lined up at the front doors at four o'clock sharp. Bruno checked their names off a list, making sure no one was trying to stay behind for a glimpse of Jean-Loup (the Scout was eventually dispatched to find two second-year boys hiding in the janitor's closet).

Seb, Frankie and Banjo sat in the student lounge playing cards and waiting for everyone to leave. Music thumped from the theater, where the student performers were rehearsing their routines for perhaps the four hundredth time.

"I'm so jealous of you guys," Camille lamented on her way to the door. "You might actually get to see him!"

Seb shook his head. "We have to go up to our rooms as soon as you leave." Frankie and Banjo nodded innocently.

"But you might bump into him," someone insisted, and Seb turned to see Murray standing near the fireplace. The boy shifted from one foot to the other, looking embarrassed. "And if you do . . . could you get me an autograph?" He held out a piece of paper.

Seb took it. "You're a fan, Murray?"

Murray nodded. "I want to join his company someday." Then he turned and hurried off.

Seb shook his head, watching him go. "Even Murray," he marveled.

A few minutes later, all the students were ushered out into the snow, and the doors shut firmly behind them.

"Finally!" Frankie tossed her cards aside. "Okay, let's get down to business."

"Right." Banjo tidied up the cards she'd just tossed. "So what happens first?"

"I can answer that," Frankie said, whipping a piece of paper out of her pocket and smoothing it on the table. "I've got a schedule of tonight's events."

Seb leaned in to see it. "Whoa! Where did you get that?"

"It was lying on the photocopier," Frankie said breezily. "What?" she added when Seb and Banjo exchanged a look. "Everyone knows that documents left lying on the photocopier are fair game."

Seb wasn't familiar with this rule, but he chose not to argue. "So what's the schedule?"

"J-Loup's flight arrives at five," Frankie reported. "They'll take him for dinner, then be back here at seven thirty for a quick tour. The show starts at eight."

"So we should head up to the choir box as soon as we can," Seb said. "We'll just bring extra food. I'll swing by the cafeteria for sandwiches."

"Don't forget the candy," said Frankie.

"I wouldn't," he assured her.

"What if someone comes looking for us?" asked Banjo. "Like, to make sure we're in our rooms?"

"They probably won't," said Frankie. "They'll all be at the show. But just in case, stuff your pillowcases with clothes, then put them under your covers so it looks like you're in there, sleeping."

"Does that really work?" Seb asked.

"Do you have a better idea?" Frankie retorted.

He didn't. And before he could come up with one, there was an enormous crash. It shook the entire school—lights swayed overhead and pictures shifted on the wall.

"Earthquake!" Banjo covered his head.

"Take cover!" Frankie scrambled behind the nearest couch.

Seb was about to follow when he saw Bruno racing past the common room, headed for the theater.

"Come on!" He jumped up and raced after him.

They stopped outside the theater doors, where a dozen teachers were huddled. Bruno pushed his way inside, but no one would let Seb through.

"What happened?" he called, standing on tiptoe but failing to see over them. He caught sight of Audrey's rainbow pants and tugged the teacher out of the scrum. "What's going on?"

"Oh, Seb." Audrey gripped his arm. "The stage collapsed! We all knew it would! It was only a matter of time . . ." She covered her mouth.

"Someone call an ambulance!" one of the teachers shouted.

"Wait, someone's hurt?" cried Seb.

Inside the theater rose a familiar wail. "They're all fine!" bellowed Angélique Saint-Germain. "Just a few scratches! The show will go on!"

And Seb knew just what had happened, even before Audrey explained.

When the old stage finally collapsed, it took the student performers down with it.

FOR A FEW minutes, Seb, Frankie and Banjo hopped around behind the teachers, trying to peek inside the theater and determine who'd been hurt. But no one would let them see. Inside, the directrice was still shouting, "The show must go on!"

"Excuse me, let me pass!" The Scout pushed his way through. "I'm trained as a paramedic!"

The crowd parted to let him pass, then closed again, only to part once more moments later as the Scout marched through with Marie-Eve in his arms. She was grimacing in pain, and her left foot stuck out at an odd angle.

"Looks like a sprain," the Scout reported as he passed. "She'll live, but she can't perform tonight. Step aside everyone, let us through."

"But maybe she can!" The directrice scurried after them. "We need a second opinion! Someone call the doctor!"

Once they were gone, the teachers closed into a huddle once more. "What are we going to do?" asked the juggling teacher.

"We need to fix the stage," said Audrey. "Or at least clean it up. Jean-Loup arrives in less than an hour—it's too late to cancel!"

"There are workers fixing pipes in the cafeteria. Someone get them!"

The teachers scattered, leaving Seb, Frankie and Banjo at the door. They peered inside at the stage—or rather, at what used to be the stage. The frame remained, but a giant hole gaped in the middle. Off to one side stood two fourth-year student trapezists, also slated to perform that night. Neither seemed hurt, but both were sniffling, consoling each other in whispers.

"I sure wouldn't want to be them," Frankie whispered.

"Do you think they'll find another tightrope act?" asked Banjo.

Before Seb could answer, Oliver Grey appeared at his side. The teacher's eyes looked weary, and his beard was flecked with lint.

"You three better go upstairs," said Oliver. "Trust me, you don't want a run-in with the directrice right now."

"But will they find a replacement for Marie-Eve?" Banjo asked.

"Not at this point," Oliver replied, peering in at the collapsed stage. "Yikes." He shook his head. "This is bad."

"One less performer won't make a huge difference though, right?" said Seb.

Oliver sighed. "We just really needed this show to go flawlessly. We have to impress Jean-Loup. He's a very powerful man with a lot of money."

"More money than God," Frankie said, with a nod to Seb.

"I guess," said Oliver.

"Have you ever been to a Terra Incognito show?" Seb asked him.

Oliver nodded. "I actually went to New York to see the

one on the skyscraper. It was definitely cool, but I always thought it could have been better if it had told a story."

"That's how I felt too," said Seb.

"So J-Loup's shows don't tell stories?" asked Frankie.

"Not usually," said Oliver.

"Hmm." Frankie's eyes narrowed.

"Anyway, you guys better make yourselves scarce. We'll take care of this mess down here."

"Okay," said Frankie. "We'll go upstairs." She pulled the boys down the hall away from the theater.

"We will?" whispered Banjo.

They turned the corner. "Of course not," said Frankie. She chose the nearest door, which happened to lead to the janitor's closet, and pulled Banjo and Seb inside. She shut the door and flicked on the light. "I have an idea."

"THAT'S INSANE," Seb told her.

"It's pretty crazy," Banjo agreed.

"It's completely *bonkers*," Seb clarified. "We are not performers. We cannot save this show."

Frankie pulled out the schedule she'd nabbed from the photocopier. "Just hear me out. This show is a big deal, and now it's missing one performance—the final performance," she added, pointing at the schedule. "And we have a performance, ready to go. And when I say we, I mean you," she added, turning to face Seb. "You've written a few of them, haven't you?"

"No!" Seb cried. "I mean, yes," he corrected himself. "But *no*, we are *not* performing them. That's crazy."

"And what's more," Frankie went on, ignoring him, "your shows tell stories. J-Loup's don't. This could make him sit up and take notice."

"So we'd just take over the stage?" Even Banjo sounded doubtful.

"Sure." Frankie looked at her schedule again. "There must be an opening somewhere."

"Frankie," Seb took a deep breath, for now she was scaring him. "There are a million things wrong with this plan. First of all, the shows I've written are just works in progress, and just for fun. I don't even know how to write a real circus show."

"But—"

"Second," he continued, "none of us are good enough to perform, especially not me."

"Well—"

"And third," he went on, "Angélique Saint-Germain would kill us for hijacking this show. Or if she let us live, she'd ship us all out first thing tomorrow. We'd be done." He stopped to catch his breath, then looked at Banjo. "Help me out here?"

Banjo chewed his lip. "It is a crazy plan—"

"Completely insane," Seb cut in.

"Would you let Banjo talk?" Frankie snapped.

"But . . . but if Jean-Loup isn't impressed by tonight's show," Banjo went on, "he won't support the school. And if Bonaventure doesn't get any more money, then we'll get shipped home anyway." He looked at his friends. "This might be our only chance."

"No!" cried Seb.

"Yes!" cried Frankie. "Come on, that scene you wrote with the animals in the zoo was really good. Let's do that."

"But I haven't finished writing it," Seb protested. "It's not even close to being ready to be performed!"

"So what if it isn't perfect?" said Frankie.

"It would be scary," Banjo admitted. "But think what might happen if we don't even try."

Seb paused, for those words sounded familiar. After a moment, he realized it was exactly what the Konstantinov fire breather had asked himself whenever he was (rightfully) frightened of spitting fuel on a flaming torch.

"He'd still have eyebrows, for one thing," Dragan had pointed out.

Dragan.

Could he help?

"Hang on," Seb told his friends. And he let himself out of the janitor's closet and ran for the common room.

★ ★ ★

"SEB!" DRAGAN CLEARLY had not expected a call. "Is everything okay?"

Seb heard the scuffle and buzz of backstage—people shouting, clown bells jingling, a sword clattering on the floor. He glanced at the clock. The Konstantinovs would have just finished their show. "I need to talk," he told his father.

"Quiet people! I need quiet!" Dragan hollered, but the clamor continued.

"Is that Seb?" someone asked. It sounded like Julie the unicyclist-in-training. "Tell him I said—"

"Not now!" Dragan roared. Then a door slammed, and all was still. "That's better."

Seb could tell his father had escaped outside, and he pictured him standing in the chilly January night, likely still wearing his top hat and ringmaster jacket. His breath would be rising into the air, maybe backlit by the moon. "Dad, I have an important question," he said. "And I don't have much time." The clock on the wall read five o'clock. Jean-Loup's plane had just landed.

"About Maxime again?" Dragan sighed.

"No," said Seb. "But he's still around, right?"

"Yes," Dragan said. "For now."

"Good. Okay." Seb drew a breath. "I want to know . . ."

He thought for a moment. "How do you know when something you've created is good enough to show the world? Or at least a small part of the world."

He heard Dragan stamp his boots on the gravel and rub his arms. "That's a good question," he said after a long pause. "A big question."

"Yes," Seb said, hoping he would sum it up quickly.

Dragan hummed and huffed, and Seb shifted from one foot to another, watching the clock tick.

"I suppose . . . ," his father said finally, "I suppose you can't know."

"What?" This was not the answer Seb needed. "There isn't, like, some kind of test?"

"Sometimes you just have to put your work out there and see what happens. You have to be brave."

"Oh." Seb swallowed. He'd been afraid of that.

"It also helps to have a good outfit," Dragan added.

"Sorry?"

"In case what you've created really is terrible," Dragan explained. "Then at least people can admire your clothes."

"I see," said Seb.

"Distract them with sequins," Dragan advised.

"Sequins," said Seb. "Got it. Thanks, Dad."

"Is that all?" Dragan asked, but Seb was already hanging up the phone.

★ ★ ★

SEB RETURNED TO the janitor's closet with his note-book. "I still think this is insane," he told his friends.

Frankie punched the air triumphantly. "Sometimes the craziest plans are the best ones," she told him.

He gave her the stink-eye.

They sat down on the floor amongst the cleaning supplies to look at his works in progress. Frankie and Banjo had seen *The Great Adventure* and even acted it out, so it made sense to go with that one.

"But I don't know if it's my best," Seb fretted, flipping through his notebook. "I've got a few others here."

"Let's see." Frankie took the notebook, and Banjo peered over her shoulder.

"They're just works—"

"In progress," Banjo finished. "We know." Then he and Frankie began to read.

Seb mauled his lower lip.

"Hey." Banjo looked up after a few minutes. "This story . . ."

Seb nodded.

Banjo went back to reading. Frankie stayed quiet, head bowed over the page.

When they reached the end, they paused for what

felt like ages to Seb, who was holding his breath. Finally, Banjo looked up again. "I think these are great," he said.

"Really?" Seb gasped, then cleared his throat. "Thanks." He turned to Frankie.

She paused for another long moment, then shrugged. "I like them."

"Really?" Seb asked again.

"No," said Frankie. She grinned. "I love them. They're our stories!"

Seb felt weak with relief. "Exactly."

Aside from *The Great Adventure*, he'd been working on two other shows.

The first starred Theo and Lily on the day they'd first met in the forest, but Seb had staged it on a high-wire. His favorite part was the surprise appearance of the bear— or rather, a performer dressed as a bear, since circus animals really had gone out of style.

The second show told the story of Cousin Luigi's wedding. Seb had created an epic battle scene using the parkour tricks and techniques Frankie had taught them. Ideally, he would stage it in a grand banquet hall, and there would be real tiramisu and minestrone soup for a full-on food fight.

In the interest of time, for it was now six o'clock, they decided to perform *The Great Adventure*—or as much of it as they could before Angélique Saint-Germain pulled them off the stage.

Frankie took out the schedule again. "Marie-Eve was supposed to perform after the trapeze act. So that'll be our chance: right before the directrice walks out to close the show, we'll take over the stage."

Seb's stomach pitched. What if the circophiles hated his show? What if Jean-Loup thought it was garbage? What if it really wasn't ready for anyone to see?

"It also helps to have a good outfit," Dragan advised in his head. "In case what you've created really is terrible."

He turned to his friends. "We need costumes."

23

SEB PEEKED AROUND the purple curtain and across the stage. He could just barely make out Frankie and Banjo, hidden in the shadows of the opposite wing. Banjo was hopping from one foot to another, and Frankie was frowning intently. Or at least Seb thought she was—it was hard to tell, since her face was mostly hidden by a massive lion's mane.

The costumes had come together surprisingly well, thanks to the costume closet where they'd hidden back in October. Frankie the lioness had her golden mane, and Banjo was sporting furry monkey ears and a long, curling tail. Seb wore a plastic elephant's trunk, which he'd attached to a piece of string wrapped around his head.

He drew back into the shadows to avoid being spotted by one of the riggers, though there wasn't much chance of that, as they were focused on the trapeze act playing out above everyone's heads. So far, it had gone flawlessly—the students were twisting and flipping and hanging off the apparatus with incredible strength and precision.

It was just too bad no one was actually watching.

The circophiles had truly outdone themselves for Jean-Loup's special soiree. Seb had seen blue lipstick and braided beards, glass slippers and cat ears. And everyone had capped off their costume with a monocle in honor of the special guest. They strutted around and preened like peacocks, as usual, but less for each other than for Jean-Loup himself.

The circus magnate was sitting near the back of the theater, on the purple velvet throne from the directrice's office. Seb had expected him to be tall and superhero-strapping like the Scout, or maybe broad-shouldered with a thick pelt of hair like Dragan. But Jean-Loup was surprisingly small, with almost delicate features. His dark hair was cropped close to his head, and Seb could make out a big bald patch on top. He looked surprisingly normal—or rather, he would have had he not been wearing an electric-blue blazer and a violet-tinted monocle.

How many monocles did the man have? Seb wondered, picturing entire closets overflowing with them. Maybe even entire castles full.

Beside Jean-Loup hovered Angélique Saint-Germain,

dressed in a floor-length crimson gown. She was pointing to the trapezists and whispering in Jean-Loup's ear, and he was nodding, though he also seemed to be stifling a yawn. Seb hoped it was due to jet lag.

Would *The Great Adventure* wake him up? Seb wondered, and his heart began to hammer. This was by far the craziest thing he'd ever done, which was really saying something for a boy who'd grown up in a circus.

He took some deep breaths and tried to focus.

The workmen had patched the stage after its collapse, but all the performers were avoiding the boards laid hastily over the giant hole. Seb had warned Frankie and Banjo to stay away from them too—if the boards gave way, they'd plummet right down into the basement, and probably break all kinds of bones.

"And we'd be trapped when the directrice came looking for us," Frankie had added darkly. Banjo had turned pale.

"Hey, this was *your* idea," Seb reminded her.

"I know," Frankie said defensively. "I'm just preparing us for the worst."

Onstage, the trapeze was rising back up to the ceiling, and the student performers were hanging sideways off it, waving good-bye to the crowd. Jean-Loup acknowledged them with a nod as he flagged down a server for more champagne. The circus magnate was looking downright bored.

"Well," Seb whispered, adjusting his trunk, "hopefully this makes him take notice."

They'd only had time to rehearse *The Great Adventure* once, in Audrey's clown classroom, before sneaking backstage. Frankie and Banjo were familiar with their parts, but Seb himself had never actually acted out any of the roles. He was having particular trouble with a simple tumbling routine near the end of the scene.

"I just can't do this, guys," he'd moaned to his friends when he ended up in a heap on the carpet.

"Yes, you can," said Frankie. "Just keep your chin tucked and shoulders strong."

"And anyway," Banjo added, "you're an elephant. You're not really meant to tumble."

This had made Seb feel slightly better—if all else failed, he would just be an elephant.

Across the stage, Frankie raised her hand to get his attention. And then, just as the stolen schedule had said it would, the lights went out in preparation for Angélique Saint-Germain's final appearance.

"This is it," Seb whispered. And he stepped out onto the dark stage.

★ ★ ★

FOR A FEW moments after the lights came back on, no one even noticed them—the circophiles were too busy chatting and stealing glances at Jean-Loup. But eventually, their chatter subsided as they spotted a monkey, a lion and an elephant on stage. A few of them giggled and pointed.

Behind his plastic trunk, Seb tried hard to get into character, to really channel his inner elephant. But the *thock* of Angélique Saint-Germain's high heels backstage was growing louder as she approached. His knees began to tremble.

She appeared in the wing he'd just left and froze at the sight of them on stage. Her hands flew to her mouth. She took a step forward, then a step back, and Seb guessed she was trying to decide which was worse: letting the bêtes noires hijack her show, or stomping out on stage to publicly wring their necks.

He decided to let her sort that out. He had a show to perform.

Banjo the monkey had already sprung himself loose from his imaginary cage, and he was tumbling around the stage, delighted with his newfound freedom. Seb watched him leap and cartwheel, and he commended himself on the casting decision: Banjo was a first-rate monkey.

While the monkey went to work on the lion's cage, Seb stole a glance at the circophiles. Some looked puzzled, others amused. Others had returned to their conversations, uninterested in the act on stage.

Once they were all free from their cages, the animals took off into the night and onto the streets of Bucharest. The lion went boldly, trying to scare off dangers with air kicks and punches. The monkey tumbled excitedly behind her. And the elephant took up the rear, inwardly questioning his decision to leave the safety of his cage for a world of uncertainty.

It quickly became clear that they needed each other. When they lost their way, the monkey scampered up the lion's back and perched on her shoulders for a better view. When an imaginary stray dog gave chase, the lion fought it off with an impressive sequence of kicks. She even threw in a flip off the stage, which made a few circophiles gasp.

And when the trio sensed approaching humans, they tossed a big tarp (also borrowed from the costume closet) over the elephant and hid underneath it together until the danger had passed.

Seb could never remember quite when it happened, but at some point, he forgot about the audience and the directrice backstage and even the possibility of getting shipped back to Eastern Europe the following day. He forgot about everyone and everything except the elephant he was pretending to be and the monkey and lion beside him. He even forgot how bad he was at acrobatics, and threw himself into his tumbling routine, which was far from perfect, but not so bad for an elephant.

It was almost as if time stood still. It was, as Maxime had said, a sense of "flow."

The scene ended with the trio running off into the Romanian countryside, uncertain where they'd end up or what adventures awaited. It wasn't exactly a happy ending, but Seb was fine with that too. It left things up to the audience's imagination, so they could make up their own stories after the show ended.

Only when Frankie gave him a good shove toward the wing did Seb come back to himself—a boy in an elephant costume who'd just hijacked a very important circus show.

"Go," she ordered. "Now."

He did as he was told, not even looking at the audience as he ran for the wing and ducked into the shadows.

"Where do we go now?" Banjo asked.

"Out the back door," said Frankie. "Follow me."

"Wait!" Seb said, for he'd heard something. "Hang on."

"No time!" Frankie snapped. "She'll be after us."

But Seb couldn't move. "Do you hear that?" he whispered.

They stopped to listen.

Out in the theater, the circophiles were applauding.

24

HE DAY AFTER the impromptu premiere of *The Great Adventure*, Seb, Frankie and Banjo found themselves once again sitting on the bench outside Angélique Saint-Germain's office, listening to Bruno pound out a concerto on his computer keyboard. No one knew quite what would happen when the directrice let them in, but all agreed it probably wouldn't be pretty.

Oliver Grey had said as much when he'd intercepted them backstage the previous night.

"You guys need to get upstairs," he'd told them. "Right now." And he'd hustled them out the back door and into the stairwell. "Stay in your rooms 'til you're told otherwise." And he'd glanced around, as if expecting the directrice to appear, on a rampage.

Banjo and Frankie took off running up the stairs, but Seb stayed back.

"Did you see it?" he had to ask.

Oliver nodded, lips pressed tightly together.

Seb braced himself for the worst. "What did you think?"

Oliver sighed. "Seb, you just hijacked a really important performance. With a modern circus show you wrote yourself."

"I know," he whispered, holding his breath.

"This is not going to go well for you," Oliver said, shaking his head. "Which is too bad, because that was a really good little show."

Seb let out his breath. "Really?"

"Really," said Oliver. "I shouldn't be proud of you, but I kind of am. But that isn't going to stop her from wringing your neck."

"I know," said Seb. But now he was grinning—he couldn't help it. His very first show was "really good."

"Go to bed," Oliver told him. "We'll talk about this tomorrow."

Seb ran upstairs, feeling equal parts terrified and elated. He'd written and performed a circus show that had made a theater of circophiles applaud. His favorite teacher was proud of him. And what's more, he was rather proud of himself.

He barely slept a wink that night, and when the Scout came to collect them all the next morning and escort them to the directrice's office, he could tell Frankie and Banjo hadn't either.

"Are you uncomfortable?" Banjo asked suddenly.

"Obviously," Frankie grumbled, shifting on the bench.

"I meant Bruno," said Banjo.

The directrice's assistant looked up from his computer.

"It's just that I think your desk is too small," said Banjo. "Maybe you should ask for a new one."

Bruno stopped typing. He looked at Banjo liked he'd never seen him before.

"He's right," Frankie chimed in. "What have you got to lose?"

"Nothing but a very small desk," said Banjo.

Before Bruno could answer, the phone on his desk rang. He picked it up, listened, then put it back down. "She's ready for you," he said. "All of you this time."

"Just think about it," Banjo advised him as they filed into the office.

Angélique Saint-Germain was seated at her whale-sized desk, in front of her wall of accomplishments. She'd changed out of her crimson gown but hadn't bothered to take off her makeup from the night before. Her lipstick was smudged and her mascara clumped, and she reminded Seb of Stanley the clown, post-performance.

They stood before her desk, shoulder to shoulder, and the directrice stared at them for a very long moment before demanding, "What on *earth* were you thinking?"

Frankie and Banjo looked at Seb. He stepped forward. "We were just trying to—"

"You were not invited to perform!" she cried. "Did I not make that clear? You . . . you misfits, you *felons* went and hijacked the most important soiree for the most important person in the entire circus world! *What were you thinking?*" she bellowed, waking Ennui, who'd been snoozing on his cushion beside her desk. The dog grunted.

"Answer me!" the directrice snapped. "Whose idea was this?"

"Mine," Seb said quickly. "Look, I—"

"Yours." The directrice's eyes locked on him. "Of course it was. How very like a Konstantinov—always needing to be in the spotlight."

"That's not true," he began.

"You are truly your father's son!"

"Well, of course I am!" Seb cried in frustration. Frankie poked him in the ribs. "Sorry," he added, and took a deep breath. "Look, I—"

"You are truly your father's son," the directrice went on. "Except, as we have established, you have no talent for performing. That show—if we can call it a show—was terrible. Abysmal. *Appalling*, even. Your form was off, all of you. Your tumbling was terrible. And *parkour*? In an acrobatics performance?" She threw her hands in the air. "What were you thinking?"

"I wanted to tell a story," Seb said quietly.

"A story?" the directrice repeated. "A *story*? Who cares about stories? What matters, as I have told you—"

Just then, the door opened and Bruno stepped inside.

"What?" she snapped.

"I have a message," he said. "I thought you should know now."

"Now?" cried the directrice. "Why now? Can't you see I'm in the middle of—" She stopped, and her eyes widened. "It's not from him, is it?"

Bruno nodded.

"*Mon Dieu.*" She clasped her hands at her heart, then beckoned for Ennui to come to her. The dog looked the other way.

"Ingrate," the directrice hissed, then turned back to Bruno. "Well, what is it? Say it quickly."

Bruno paused for a long moment, and Seb could have sworn he saw the corners of his mouth twitch. Was Bruno enjoying this? he wondered.

"He's going to donate," said Bruno.

The bêtes noires gasped.

"I knew it!" Angélique Saint-Germain tore at her hair. "I knew he'd drive me back into hiding and tar my reputation—" She paused. "Wait, he's what?"

"He *is*?" Banjo exclaimed.

Frankie cursed in Italian.

Now Bruno couldn't hide his smile. "Jean-Loup said he enjoyed the show last night. *Especially* the last performance."

"He *did*?" Seb's mouth fell open.

Bruno nodded. "He said he appreciated the story. In fact, it's inspired a new idea for a Terra Incognito show, in which he plans to set some circus animals free, back into the wild. It's a statement about the modern circus," Bruno added. "He hasn't worked out the details yet."

Frankie swore again, this time in French.

"Anyway," Bruno went on, "he's going to send us a check."

"A check," the directrice whispered. "For . . . how much?"

"Let's discuss that later," Bruno said, nodding at Seb and his friends. "But it's a significant sum."

For a moment, Angélique Saint-Germain sat very still, staring into the middle distance. Then her gaze snapped back to the bêtes noires. "Leave us," she told them. "Now."

They didn't have to be told twice.

★ ★ ★

"SEBASTIAN." THE SCOUT tapped him on the shoulder. "Phone call for you."

Seb looked up from his math homework, which he'd been doing in the student lounge. "For me?"

The Scout nodded, then strolled away, smiling.

Seb jogged over to the phone and picked it up. "Hello?"

"Sebastian," said Dragan Konstantinov. "I have an important question for you."

"Dad!" Seb exclaimed. His father had never once called him at school. "Is everything okay?"

Seb heard a scuffle on Dragan's end, then his father snapped, "Would you give me some space? I am talking to my son!"

"All right, all right," muttered Stanley the clown.

"Seb," Dragan said again, and Seb steeled himself for bad news. "I received a call from Angélique Saint-Germain just now."

"Oh!" Seb sighed with relief. "Right. She said she was going to call you."

"And she did," said his father. "She called me to sing your praises, to tell me about your intelligence and creativity! Sebastian," he said seriously, "is the woman all right? I mean, is she *all there*?"

Seb had to laugh.

269

"She said you had the makings of a future circus director! That you created a brilliant show that knocked the monocle off Jean-Loup! *Jean-Loup!* Is this true?"

"I guess so." Seb grinned.

For a moment, Dragan fell silent. Then he let out a whoop. Somewhere behind him, all the Konstantinovs began cheering as well. Bells jingled. A horn honked.

"*Bravo!*" cried Maxime. "*Bravo, Seb!*"

Seb's mouth was starting to hurt from smiling. It had started that morning, when the Scout delivered a note from Angélique Saint-Germain, written on nice, heavy cardstock that was smooth to the touch. It read:

Sebastian Konstantinov, Francesca de Luca
and Banjo Brady:

You are welcome to apply for early admission to your
second year at the Bonaventure Circus School. This is a
privilege reserved for only the most promising students.
We hope you will accept this offer and stay with us
another year, continuing to work hard and contribute
your unique talents to our world-class circus school.

Sincerely,
Angélique Saint-Germain
P.S.: You are, of course, no longer on probation.

"I'm proud of you, Seb," said Dragan.

"Thanks, Dad," said Seb.

"I wonder . . ." his father went on. "I mean, if it doesn't interfere with your schoolwork, perhaps you could . . ." He paused and cleared his throat. Seb waited. "Perhaps you could start working on a show . . . for the Konstantinovs. Something we could tackle when you come home this summer?"

"Yes!" Seb practically shouted. "Of course! I'll get on it right away."

"Just . . ." Dragan lowered his voice. "Just make sure there's a ringmaster in it."

"I will," Seb promised. "But Dad—" He glanced behind him, where Frankie and Banjo had appeared in the doorway, dressed in winter coats and mitts. "I've got to go, okay? My English teacher is taking us to Mont Royal to go sledding."

"Who's us?" asked Dragan.

"My friends." Seb grinned again. "The bêtes noires."

He hung up the phone, then ran to join them.

La Fin

ACKNOWLEDGMENTS

UN GRAND MERCI to all who helped in the making of this novel, whether by listening to me ramble on about the modern circus, accompanying me to shows on various continents, reading incoherent first drafts or even bravely attempting to teach me circus acrobatics. I am deeply indebted and still mildly bruised.

Special thanks to:

Lynne Missen, the greatest editor I could hope for and a wonderful human as well, and the entire team at Penguin Random House Canada.

Marie Campbell, for championing my work, believing in the worlds and characters I dream up and for thoughtful and savvy advice.

Vikki VanSickle, Tanya and Julia Kyi, Kallie George, Zoe Grames-Webb and Louise Delaney, for being astute and amenable first readers.

My circus mentors, especially the remarkable Natalie Parkinson-Dupley at Toronto's Hercinia Arts Collective, Duncan Wall, Lori Sherritt-Fleming and the crews at Cirque-ability and the Vancouver Circus School. (I do want to note, however, that while I did pester various circus pros at various schools, Bonaventure and all those in it are creations of my imagination, not based on anyone or any place I encountered.)

And finally, wholeheartedly, to the Canada Council for the Arts, the Toronto Arts Council, and the Access Copyright Foundation for supporting my work and that of so many Canadian artists. We truly could not do what we do without you.